The crosshairs were fixed now. Mitchell began the steady increase in pressure on the trigger which could have only one conclusion.

At the moment that his finger flew back and met the trigger guard, Mitchell recognized the face that filled the scope.

And it was in that fraction of a second that the skull of the man on the left was shattered by a bullet from a high-powered rifle that raised him from his seat and flung him across the corner of the table into a lifeless mass on the floor.

Mitchell lowered the scope, a look of bewildered horror on his face.

"Oh, my God!" he mumbled as, sighting the scope again, he verified what he knew he had seen.

THE MAN ON THE LEFT

WAYNE J. GARDINER

CHARTER
NEW YORK

A DIVISION OF CHARTER COMMUNICATIONS INC.
A GROSSET & DUNLAP COMPANY

First Charter Printing January 1981
Published simultaneously in Canada
Manufactured in the United States of America

2 4 6 8 0 9 7 5 3 1

*To my wife Kathy, for
her help and support*

Prologue

David Mitchell was sprawled face down on the jungle floor, his nose pressed against the muddied earth. The man beside him was dead.

A fly droned lazily near Mitchell's ear and landed on his cheek. It crawled slowly across his mouth and down to his chin, then back again. Mitchell didn't move. After a moment, the fly buzzed off.

Mitchell remained in the exact position he had maintained for over a half-hour . . . the position into which he had fallen when the AK-47 slug knocked him to the ground. It was only a flesh wound, grazing his chest. It burned like fire and bled profusely for several minutes, soaking his fatigue shirt in a mixture of blood and sweat. While the wound was not serious, it produced results that looked grave indeed.

From the corner of his eye, Mitchell saw the butt of his rifle. It had bounced from his grasp when he fell and slid downhill under a bush some twenty feet away.

He was the only one of four members of a 9th Infantry Division long range reconnaissance patrol still alive.

It had been a well-laid ambush. It was not something that was supposed to happen to an elite long range reconnaissance patrol. They were not out to engage the enemy. They would in fact, go to any length to avoid it. If the circumstances had permitted, they would all have been highly embarrassed.

Instead, they were all dead, save Mitchell. And his prospects for living were certainly in doubt.

The bodies were scattered across fifty yards of heavily vegetated forest. Just ahead of them was a small clearing, no more than thirty yards square, the landing zone at which they were to be picked up shortly after nightfall.

They had been dropped there two nights earlier. The chopper had skimmed in at tree-top level, then swooped into the small clearing, hovering a few feet above ground while the four jumped out. They hit the ground running. Before they had reached the cover at the edge of the forest, the helicopter was gone. They ran to the west, as fast as the terrain and darkness would allow, for a full hour before stopping to rest and collect their bearings. Satisfied that they had made a secure landing they located their position on a terrain map, and shooting an azimuth with the magnetic compass, set off at an easier rate toward the southwest.

The first critical element of a successful reconnaissance patrol had been met. They had cleared the drop area safely. But their arrival had not gone unnoticed. A local Viet Cong patrol had heard the helicopter from a hilltop a quarter of a mile away. Through binoculars, they watched the silhouette of the whirling rotors against the night sky. They moved off quickly in that direction, hoping to catch the men who had jumped from the helicopter by surprise. They moved cautiously but purposefully through what was familiar ground to them.

Within minutes, they stood at the landing site. They had seen no sign of the patrol. They had obviously cleared the area. It was pointless, and perhaps dangerous, to try to pick up their trail and pursue them in darkness.

On the other hand, there was a reasonable possibility

that the men who had been dropped would be picked up later in the night, or perhaps within the next few days. Patience was a virtue the VC had in abundance. They were in no hurry. Their tour of duty wouldn't be over in a year. They were there for the duration.

They prepared an ambush site before dawn and settled down to wait.

The attack had been swift and deadly. A killing crossfire raked the forty yard interval between the point man and the last man in the file. Instinctively as the first shot screamed overhead, they lurched for cover. Within seconds, the fusillade of fire that tore into the earth and ripped through trees and shrubs and bodies fell quiet. The victims had never seen their attackers. They had not fired a single shot in defense.

The sun shone fully on Mitchell's back. He strained to hear any sound that might tell him where the enemy was. But the only noise was the deceptively tranquil hum of insects in the thick jungle air. Mitchell wondered for a moment if they had moved on.

Then—through half-closed eyes—a movement in the distance.

Mitchell watched as a young Viet Cong soldier padded warily toward them. Sent forward to verify their deaths, he appeared nervous and hurried. Mitchell prayed that his distress would be so great that he would take Mitchell for dead. It was Mitchell's only hope of survival.

The black-clad soldier prodded at the two bodies some eighty feet away with the muzzle of his rifle and with his sandaled feet. He picked up their weapons and took some personal effects from their bodies. When he left them and headed toward Mitchell, Mitchell closed his eyes and took a deep breath and braced himself to take whatever might come. His heart pounded so furiously that he feared it might be heard.

The VC kicked Mitchell tentatively in the ribs, then rolled him face-up with a foot. He ripped the watch from Mitchell's wrist. The watchband cut into Mitchell's flesh, but the set expression on Mitchell's face didn't change.

The VC untied Mitchell's boots and jerked them off his feet. He spent a futile moment searching for Mitchell's weapon, then moved on to the last man.

Minutes later, carrying all he could handle, he retraced his steps. Mitchell heard him moving off into the brush behind him.

Mitchell breathed more easily and sought to bring his heartbeat back under control.

He could hear them talking now, several voices jabbering at once. The voices drew nearer. Then, through half-closed eyes, he saw them approaching. He counted them as they moved out of the dense foliage. Eight. All armed with rifles.

What might happen now was anyone's guess. Mitchell had heard the stories of mutilation. Beads of perspiration formed on his brow and began to run down his cheek.

The VC patrol stopped near the first two bodies. They pointed and gestured and talked for a moment and then moved on.

Mitchell realized with a sickening feeling that dead men didn't sweat. It would cost him his life if the VC noticed it.

It didn't seem fair, he thought. It wouldn't be fair to die because of a circumstance he couldn't control.

Through narrowed eyes, he watched them approach. He held his breath and his body tensed, ready to make whatever final attempt might be required to survive.

They walked past him, less than ten yards away, with scarcely a glance.

The patrol walked to the edge of the clearing where they stopped and began to talk again. Mitchell could identify the leader by his actions. He was a short but powerfully built man with a high-pitched voice. He pointed at the small open area and then at a cluster of thick bushes twenty yards across the clearing. They talked for a few more moments and then four of the men split from the group and crossed the clearing. Mitchell watched as they took up positions at appropriate intervals in the bushes. The four who stayed in position near Mitchell also took cover, facing the clearing, their backs to him.

The Viet Cong knew that the return of the recon patrol to the landing zone meant that a helicopter would be back soon to claim them. They would wait for it to arrive.

Mitchell's only chance to get out alive was to see that the helicopter left safely—with him on it. He made mental notes of each enemy soldier's position. He marked them with prominent features that he would be able to identify in darkness. He formulated a plan. He would have to wait until darkness to carry it out.

The shadows of the tree tops stretched further across the ground. Mitchell remained motionless, but breathed easier now. He had more time than he wanted to reflect on the fate of the others.

He could see Tim Browning well. He was the nearest to him. His body had been riddled with bullets.

Further down the line, Cross and Fredericks lay, twisted grotesquely in death.

There was time now for the reality of their deaths to sink in. The fact that he was alive moved him. It was almost ironic. He had ten days to go until his tour of duty expired. He had received his orders two weeks earlier. He would be assigned to Ft. Sheridan, Illinois, near Chicago. It was an assignment he looked forward to with great anticipation. He wondered if he would ever get there.

His emotions ran the gamut between hope and despair. At one moment he knew he was invincible—knew that in ten days he would be on a plane lifting out of Tan Son Nhut Airbase, cheering wildly as the lights of Saigon faded in the distance. He could taste the incredible feeling of elation.

In the next moment, he despaired, knowing in his very soul that he wouldn't live to see the end of the day. The odds were insurmountable. The realization overwhelmed him.

He became angry. Angry at the rag-tag, rubber-sandaled, pajama wearing slopes that wouldn't allow him to fulfill the destiny of his life.

Browning, Cross and Fredericks. Dead.

He shouldn't have volunteered for the mission. What the hell was he thinking of! Ten days left. He could easily have spent it at division headquarters. No one expected him to go on patrol. No one would have asked him. But they had needed a military intelligence expert. Someone who could evaluate the reported large scale troop movements from an intelligence perspective. Mitchell had wanted to go. He liked the freedom and solitude that the long range reconnaissance patrols provided.

Browning, Cross and Fredericks.

How many other names could he add to that list? He didn't want to consider it. Most had been good men.

He corrected himself. All were good men—they were dead now, give them the benefit of the doubt. Men with people who loved them . . . with destinies . . . with children to father and raise.

Browning . . . and Cross . . . and. . . .

Suddenly, he wanted to cry. It was an almost overpowering feeling that welled up and threatened to burst out. The rush of emotion surprised him. After a year's time, and all he had been through, he thought he had become immune to it. He struggled to maintain control. He reminded himself that he was a military intelligence officer in the United States Army. He was a professional soldier. This was a matter of life and death . . . life and death. . . .

Behind him, the sun began to sink below the horizon. He brought his thoughts back to the matter at hand. The enemy was deployed for the ambush. They waited patiently in position. They were very quiet . . . very disciplined.

The sun set and the long shadows fused into a solid gray that became steadily darker as the minutes dragged on.

In another hour, the darkness was nearly complete. Mitchell moved his stiffened muscles for the first time since the attack. He rolled over slowly on his side and felt the wound on his chest. It had stopped bleeding long ago and his bloodied tee shirt was stuck to his chest. He left it at that. It wasn't serious and it wouldn't hinder him.

He felt inside the flapped pocket of his jungle fatigue shirt and closed his hand around the two grenades he carried there. When he had fallen, their weight in the loosely fitting garment had settled them down at his side. His arm partially concealed them when the young Viet Cong soldier had come forward. He hadn't noticed them. It would prove to be a fatal mistake.

As the darkness became total, Mitchell knew that time was short. At varying stages in the transformation from day to night, he reverified the terrain features that marked the positions of the four men across the clearing. His life depended on whether they remained in those positions.

Mitchell crawled down to the bush and groped in the

darkness for his rifle. It was covered with mud and the barrel was plugged. Mitchell brushed it and poked it and scraped it with twigs and grass to clean it up.

He didn't have as much time as he wanted. In the distance he heard the faint echo of helicopter rotors cutting the night air. He couldn't worry about whether the weapon was ready to fire.

He scrambled back up the slope and inched closer to the four men nearest him. He knew their positions well. He worked his way behind a bush only ten feet from the nearest one. He could see all four in the faint light. They were intent on the sound of the helicopter that was approaching from the front. He heard the leader issue a command to the others.

Mitchell took the grenades from his pocket an pulled both pins. He stood behind the bush and heaved them quickly, one after the other, on a line with the tree tops that he had singled out across the small clearings.

The throws had to be perfect. He heard them crash through the foliage.

Startled voices from across the clearing. Seconds later, the white light of explosion and the familiar concussion that sent lethal fragments of metal spraying through the air. Men screamed.

There was movement ahead of him. Mitchell charged through the bush screaming. He fired eight bursts of automatic fire. The four men with their backs to him were dead before they could turn around.

He emptied the rest of his magazine across the clearing, then reloaded.

It was quiet.

Only the sound of the helicopter. Just over the hill.

Mitchell ran into the middle of the clearing.

Suddenly the chopper popped into view. It flashed a light once into the clearing. Mitchell waved frantically. The big machine dropped into the opening. The doors were open and the pilots, eyes glazed from the strain of their incredible job, yelled at Mitchell to board.

The intense roar of the engine drowned out the sound of the single rifle that barked out from across the clearing. But scarcely a foot in front of him, Mitchell heard the splat and saw metal fly as a bullet slammed into the side of the aircraft. The door gunner saw the muzzle flash. He instantly whirled the M-60 machine gun on its swivel and poured a deadly volume of fire into the trees. There was no answering fire.

"Get in!" yelled the pilot.

Mitchell stuck his head in the door and yelled back to be heard. "There are more of us! I need help getting them back!"

"Are they wounded?"

"Dead!" called Mitchell.

"Leave them! Let's get our asses out of here. We're sitting ducks!"

Mitchell couldn't believe what he'd heard. "I won't leave them!" he bellowed. "The VC are dead. There were only eight of them. We're not in danger. You have to help me pick my men up!"

"We're not a med-evac unit!" yelled the pilot. "We're leaving!" He revved the engine.

Mitchell gritted his teeth and thrust the muzzle of his weapon inside the helicopter. "If you try to pull this fucking thing out of here without them, I'll shoot it down, so help me God!"

The co-pilot looked at Mitchell, then at the pilot. "He means it," he said.

The pilot nodded. "He's crazier than we are," he said. "All right!" he yelled to one of the door runners. "Give him a hand!"

They waited nervously while Mitchell and the machine gunner brought back the bodies. In a few moments they were airborne, skimming the tree tops in a dizzying roller-coaster ride back to the divisional base camp.

Browning, Cross, Fredericks and Mitchell. All were accounted for.

Mitchell left for the U.S. on schedule. He didn't cheer when the big Pan Am jet lifted off the runway in Saigon. It didn't seem fair. There were too many left behind.

When the Third Battalion commander heard Mitchell's story, he wanted to recommend Mitchell for a citation. Mitchell didn't want it. He might have felt differently if the others had gotten back alive.

Nonetheless, the request was put through. Three months later at Ft. Sheridan, the post commander pinned a Silver Star on Mitchell's chest.

Mitchell's estimated time in service date came up eight months later. He contacted the personnel office in Washington to try and get an indication of what his next assignment would be.

The letter he received in return was very blunt. "Military Intelligence captains who have been in the states over six months should expect to return to Vietnam for another tour."

"That's a little too soon for me," said Mitchell. He resigned his commission.

A few months later he had taken a job and was almost beginning to think of himself as a civilian.

As time passed, he reached the point where he scarcely flinched at loud noises. He settled into a routine of life that left the Army far behind.

Ten years later, he had nearly forgotten it.

Chapter 1.

It was 3:15 in the morning. On the ninth floor of a Washington, D.C. hotel room, two men sat facing each other across a small wooden table. The man nearest the window had been talking for over a half hour but he was finished now and waited for the other to respond. They sat in silence for several minutes, but the man nearest the window didn't press for an answer. When he saw that none was immediately forthcoming, he pushed his black leather chair away from the table, moved quietly to the window and stood staring absently into the park across the street. The man seated at the table remained deep in thought.

It was the 29th day of March, 1979, and it was a balmy night in Washington. The breeze that wafted through the open window carried the hint of swelling cherry blossoms, straining to burst into bloom. Within the week, the explosion of pink would take place and thousands of visitors from across the nation would come to witness the annual spectacle.

But the two men in the hotel room weren't concerned with this.

The man at the window was tall and lean, standing six-foot-four and weighing just under two hundred pounds. His features were handsome and well-defined. The slight graying at the temples didn't detract from his impressive countenance, but rather, enhanced it. He was in remarkable physical condition for a man of forty-eight years. He stood ramrod straight, looking out the window with ice-blue eyes that characteristically searched and penetrated.

Outside the traffic lights blinked alternately in yellow and red and it was quiet. Only an occasional car passed on the street below.

The man seated at the table shifted in his chair and cleared his throat. He was older than the tall man, sixty-two years, and his physical presence was not nearly as imposing. Yet despite a receding hairline and a considerable paunch, there was an air of confidence about him. The furrows in his brow attested to years of thoughtful decision making. He wasn't an impulsive man, and he spoke in a deliberate, measured manner.

"And you're sure there's no other alternatve?"

The tall man turned away from the window. His voice sounded exactly as one might expect . . . crisp, decisive, and directly to the point.

"None!" he said.

"No alternatives at all?"

"No acceptable alternatives, sir." He crossed to the table and took a seat.

The older man eyed him thoughtfully. For all the respect he had for this man, he couldn't help disliking him. Too confident, he thought. Always so absolutely assured. In a way, he envied him. At the same time, he was too practical to let personal feelings influence his thought. He needed men like this and he knew it.

"This is one hell of a big step, Walker," he said.

The tall man's expression remained passive. He nodded in agreement. They sat in silence again.

When the older man finally spoke, it was in an abrupt manner. "We'll do it!"

Obvious approval registered on the face of the man called Walker. "It's the only thing we can do, sir."

"Well, then . . . let's get on to a rather important point." He settled back in the chair and crossed his legs. "Who's going to perform the mission?"

Walker leaned over the table and snapped open the briefcase that rested next to his chair. There was a single brown envelope inside. Opening it, he took out a manila folder and slid it across the table.

The older man edged forward in his chair and studied the file. "He's not one of our regular men?"

"I thought it would be better that way." Walker took a cigarette, lit it and inhaled deeply. "He's perfect for it, sir. He's the ideal man. The fact he's not associated with us can only work to our advantage."

The other looked back into the file. "He *is* qualified," he said at last.

Walker took a drag on his cigarette and a wisp of blue smoke tailed off into the air. "Sir, I've checked literally hundreds through the computer." He motioned to the file. "That man is ideally suited."

"What if he won't accept?" the older man asked.

"He'll accept, sir. I've memorized that file. I know that man as well as he knows himself . . . maybe better." He flicked the ash off the end of his cigarette. "He'll accept."

"Let's just suppose, Walker," the older man persisted, "that through some quirk he doesn't agree. What then?"

"We have a few alternatives, just in case," Walker admitted. "But we won't need them."

"And if we explain this thing and he refuses . . . what about the security aspect?"

Walker looked across the table and into the eyes of

the older man. "Well, sir," he intoned, "that's one of those situations we'd have to adapt to at the time."

The room was quiet again and the older man went back to the folder. A gust of wind swept the drapes out and gently rustled the papers in the open file.

The older man stood up and looked at his watch. "Go ahead with it then, Walker." He put his coat on and started for the door. "I'm glad you brought this to my attention as soon as it developed." He laid the folder on the table.

"Thank you for coming, sir," Walker said, standing. "I know it's a little irregular this way, but under the circumstances I thought any departure from normal procedure might be wise."

The older man laughed. He was finally at ease after having made his decision. "You were right as usual, Walker. No one would expect to find me here, particularly at this time of night."

They smiled and shook hands.

"Keep me informed, Walker. Good night."

"Good night, sir," Walker said.

The older man opened the door and two husky young men in non-descript but well-tailored suits immediately appeared outside. They scanned the hallway in both directions, then motioned him out. Together they walked down the hallway to the rear stairwell.

A compact size Chevrolet, chosen for its non-descript appearance, picked them up. It was not a car normally associated with the office of the man who climbed inside. They drove off quickly in the direction of Pennsylvania Avenue.

Walker closed the door and methodically began to put the room in order. He glanced at his watch. Four o'clock. When the maids came to clean the room in the morning they'd find a bed unslept in, a room unspoiled.

They wouldn't think much of it, other than to be thankful for one less job to do. They would never know that the previous night, two men had formulated plans in that unimpressive room that would effect the entire world.

Frank Walker laid the key on the table, picked up the manila folder and studied it thoughtfully. A single blue tab was centered on the folder. Typewritten across the tab was simply:

MITCHELL, DAVID R.
581-42-8670

He slipped the folder into the envelope, placed the envelope into the briefcase and locked it. A moment later he closed the door behind him, took the stairs to the basement and left the building through the garage.

Chapter 2.

You could never really say that Apartment 8-B was spotlessly clean. In fact, it would be charitable to refer to it on its best days as "comfortable." On this particular morning, it was in a little more disarray than usual.

Inside, Dave Mitchell had just gotten out of bed and found himself severely hung over. He crossed to the window and jerked open the drapes. He winced as bright sunlight flooded in.

It was the last day of March in Chicago and stubborn traces of an unseasonably late snowstorm had finally disappeared. Mitchell opened the window widely, squinting to adjust his eyes to the brilliantly clear day.

Across the street, Lincoln Park, in the midst of its annual transition from the drab brown cover of winter to the lively green of spring, sprawled out before him. A large Saturday crowd was out in force to take advantage of the mild weather. Their shouts and laughter were carried on gentle gusts of wind that blew off Lake Michigan. He stood at the window and looked far out across the lake.

Dave Mitchell looked older than his thirty-five years, with a serious, handsome face. Long blonde hair curled slightly over his collar and intense blue eyes complemented a fair complexion. The muscles that had once been in perfect tone had begun to sag slightly over the past few years.

He had a sense of humor but certainly didn't overwork it. Those who knew him characterized him as a "no-nonsense" type. He had a certain restlessness in his manner. He was a skeptic and a pessimist, despite the successes he'd achieved in almost every endeavor he'd undertaken.

By anyone's standard, Dave Mitchell should have been a contented, self-satisfied individual. He was aware of all that, but it made little difference to him.

Mitchell tightened the belt of his blue terrycloth bath robe and turned away from the window. In his hand he held several letters and a newspaper he had picked up from his mailbox in the lobby downstairs. He hadn't bothered to look at them yet.

He threw the mail on the dining room table and pushed through the swinging shuttered doors into the kitchen. The sink was piled high with dishes and Mitchell wrinkled his nose at the odor that hung in the room.

He walked to the refrigerator and stood briefly, studying his distorted reflection in the metal trim. He leaned his forehead against the refrigerator and closed his eyes. The pleasant coolness spread mercifully across his brow and momentarily eased the throbbing in his head. He thought about promising himself he'd never drink that much again, but found he wasn't sufficiently motivated to do anything that drastic.

He looked critically around the kitchen and shook his head. It hadn't been like this when Jeannie was there. She'd have a fit if she saw it now. Mitchell laughed at the thought. The one domestic task she took seriously was housecleaning. Any comparisons between her and a typical *Ladies Home Journal* reader ended there. The price had been a little too high to pay for a clean kitchen.

At their first meeting, Jean Fenner had impressed her future husband as a spoiled and snooty bitch from Chicago's north shore suburbs. Less than a week later, that objective viewpoint flew out the window at the exact moment they leapt into bed for the first time.

Now, four years later, and three months from the final divorce papers, Mitchell could admit what he'd known all along—his original assessment had been correct.

She had spent nearly four years proving it. She was a beautiful woman with an air of elegance that she overplayed far too much. She was very aware of her beauty and used it well. She knew the effect it had on men. If someone didn't react in the manner she was conditioned to expect, she considered it not only an affront, but a personal challenge.

Dave Mitchell had presented her with such a challenge. He wondered how many others she had influenced with the same technique she used on him.

The thought of it occupied more of his time than was healthy. And while his nagging doubts were based in fact, her actions almost certainly were not at the epidemic proportions that he imagined them.

Mitchell was not entirely blameless himself. He was not one to take such treatment without retaliation. The opportunity, of course, was always there. The business lunches became more casual and lasted longer. The need for entertaining in the evening became more pressing. The planning sessions were more frequent and lasted well into the night.

Within three years, the trust had eroded entirely from their marriage. They hung on for another year, probably because they didn't know what else to do.

He came home one night to find her gone.

Though he had expected it to happen eventually, the act of her leaving hit him harder than he had imagined it would. He went from surprise to hurt to bitter. It galled him that she had been the one to leave. Throughout their relationship, they had been just about even in gamesmanship. Now she was one up on him.

Mitchell embarked on a non-stop party that lasted over two months. He threw himself into his work with an uncommon zeal, determined to show her that he would be even more successful without her.

Finally he realized he was being asinine. The partying was killing him and he wasn't having that much fun. And he was beating his brains out in a job that he already excelled in and really didn't care about anyway.

He backed down from his theme of venegeance and began to enjoy his freedom.

It felt good. He forgot about her.

Mitchell took a glass from the cabinet above the sink and opened the refrigerator. He filled the glass with ice cubes, took a bottle of tomato juice and closed the door. From a half-filled bottle of vodka on the counter beside the sink, Mitchell splashed a healthy shot into his glass and filled it with tomato juice. "Just a little eye-opener," he said aloud.

From there, he made his way into the living room where he sank into the sofa. The sun shone warmly through the window and stretched across the floor of the room.

For fifteen minutes Dave Mitchell sat contentedly, methodically draining his glass, thinking about nothing in particular. The bloody mary was doing wonders for a head that, only an hour earlier, he thought would never return to normal. He finished the last of it and went into the bathroom where he shaved and then forced himself to stand for five minutes under a miserably cold shower.

Back in the living room he picked up the empty glass from the cocktail table in front of the sofa, took it into the kitchen, and added it to the mountainous pile in the sink. Then he went down the hallway to the bedroom threw his robe on the floor, crawled into bed and was asleep in two minutes.

It was after four o'clock when he woke up. The steady pounding had left his head and the queasy feeling had gone from his stomach. He went to the kitchen where he managed to uncover a pan from the rubble in the sink, washed it and warmed a can of ravioli on the stove. The third round of the Sea Pines Heritage Classic was on TV and Mitchell tuned in just as Tom Watson rolled in a twenty-foot birdie putt to take a two stroke lead on the field.

He sat in the easy chair and ate the ravioli. Before the round ended, Watson had added two more and held a four stroke advantage going into the final eighteen holes on Sunday. The outcome, thought Mitchell, was inevitable. Watson with a four shot lead made for a very anti-climactic final round.

He thumbed through the *TV Guide* as Vin Scully reminded everyone to tune in on Sunday for the climactic final round.

The mail on the table caught his eye. Mitchell gathered it in one hand and transferred it to the end table beside the easy chair. A pile of record albums were stacked above the turntable inside the stereo cabinet. He grabbed the first several off the top, flipped the switch and dropped into the chair. The strains of a Dave Brubeck album filled the room.

There were a total of four letters. Three were addressed to "Occupant." Mitchell crumpled them individually and threw them in the general direction of the waste basket in the far corner of the room. The fourth letter was addressed to him and was marked, "Department of the Army, Official Business." With an appropriate comment on junk mail, he laid it aside for the moment.

He picked up the *Tribune* and leafed slowly through it. The lead story was on an airline accident in Brazil that had claimed sixty-eight lives, including two members of the U.S. Consulate in Brasilia; in West Germany, Chancellor Karl Stehlin dismissed the recent increase in incidents of civil disturbance as "merely the right of free individuals to express themselves;" and from the Scottsdale, Arizona, training camp of the Chicago Cubs, Ernie Banks predicted a pennant in '79.

Finally he got back to the letter. At first glance, it was like any one of several he'd received since leaving the Army. There had been notifications of changes in VA benefits, changes in reserve status, discharges and a host of other things he'd scarcely bothered to read. But Mitchell noticed two unusual things before he opened it.

The return address in the top left corner wasn't Veterans Administration, St. Louis, as it normally was. Rather, the return was marked "OPAIS, Washington."

Army Intelligence and Security had been his service branch, but all the correspondence he'd received from the army during the past several years had come from the VA. Mitchell was mildly curious as to why he was hearing now from the AIS Personnel Office.

The other unusual feature was not a change in what normally appeared on an envelope, but rather, an omission. There was no postage cancellation indicating when and from where the letter was sent.

He flipped his wrist and snapped open the folded sheet of paper.

WAYNE J. GARDINER

DEPARTMENT OF THE ARMY
OFFICE OF PERSONNEL, ARMY
INTELLIGENCE SECURITY
THE PENTAGON
WASHINGTON, D.C.

30 March 79

SUBJECT: Special Assignment

TO: CPT MITCHELL, DAVID R.
    581-42-8670 MI VETERAN
    2410 N. LINCOLN PARK WEST
    CHICAGO, ILL. 60614

1. AIS has been charged with responsibility for performing a mission vital to U.S. security.

2. A review of available records indicates you are qualified to take part in this mission.

3. You will be contacted with further details within one (1) week.

4. Information regarding this mission is highly confidential and should be handled as such.

BY ORDER OF THE PRESIDENT OF THE UNITED STATES:

        IRWIN GORDON
        MAJ MI
        OIC, OPAIS

DISTRIBUTION:

1 - The President of the United States
1 - Mitchell, David R.
1 - Project File

He read the letter three times before he laid it face up on the table.

Mitchell didn't know exactly what to make of it. He looked at the bottom left-hand corner of the letter again. "BY ORDER OF THE PRESIDENT OF THE UNITED STATES." That was not particularly unusual. Literally hundreds of letters dispatched from the army carry that line. It was the last item that intrigued him:

DISTRIBUTION:

1 - The President of the United States
1 - Mitchell, David R.
1 - Project File

Pretty select company. He mulled it over for several minutes.

". . . highly confidential and should be handled as such."

The missing postmark meant the letter had been delivered by some means other than regular mail service. If the subject were really as sensitive as it appeared it might be, that departure from normal procedure would make sense.

". . . highly confidential and should be handled as such."

He folded the letter and placed it into the envelope. From a drawer in the kitchen, Mitchell took a screwdriver and roll of Scotch tape and went into the bedroom. He knelt at the base of the wall opposite the bed, removed two screws from a gray vent cover and pulled it free. He blew some of the puffy, standing lint down into the duct and rubbed the sides clean with a handkerchief. Then he attached strips of tape to three sides of the envelope, extending them over the edge a half inch. Reaching down inside the vent, Mitchell pressed the overlapped tape to the side of the duct, fixing the envelope firmly in place. The top of the envelope was free of tape, allowing the letter to be removed and replaced without disturbing its secure resting place. Mitchell repositioned the cover and tightened the two screws. He stood over the vent and inspected his work.

The thought he might be making an ass of himself crossed his mind. He didn't deny the possibility. But he had decided it wouldn't do any harm to play it safe. Besides, he admitted, it was the most intrigued he'd been about anything in years.

It was after six o'clock now and the sun was low in the west. Outside the warmth of day was disappearing with the sunlight. It was that transitional period between the day's activities and the Saturday night social circuit and it was quiet on the street.

Mitchell dressed and left the apartment and walked to one of the neighborhood pubs on Clark Street. Only a small group of regulars was gathered at that hour. Several of them called Mitchell by name.

He had a sandwich and spent nearly two hours there, drinking and shooting pool, before taking a cab to Rush Street.

By eight-thirty, there was an unusually large crowd on the near north side. At the popular spots, long lines formed on the sidewalks outside where college dropouts with seventeen inch collars checked I.D.'s.

Mitchell forged his way inside Butch's Tavern.

For several hours he completely forgot about the letter. But as the night wore on, and the liquor began to take effect, it worked its way back into his mind. Mitchell found himself recounting the letter word for word and his memory replayed the four years he'd spent in the army, from start to finish and back again.

They had been good years, as satisfying as anything he'd done. He'd never felt a greater sense of responsibility, a greater awareness of the importance of what he was doing, a greater awareness of life itself. What the hell, he finally admitted, he had loved it. The bad times had faded from memory with the passing years. It was difficult now to remember why he left.

Mitchell shook his head with a twinge of regret. He was making decisions now about which jingle to use to sell a new bar of soap and what kind of catchy name they could come up with for a new feminine hygiene deodorant. Back then, he'd been making decisions that influenced life and death . . . life and death. . . .

Mitchell lost count of the drinks. He killed the one in his hand and ordered another.

He wasn't aware of the time until two o'clock. The lights were suddenly on in the bar and Mitchell found himself being carried toward the front door by the steady current of moving bodies. As they spilled out onto the street, he realized he'd had more than enough to drink. He took a cab straight back to his apartment.

"Thanks, troop," he said as he paid the driver. Mitchell saluted as the cab pulled away. He leaned gratefully against the back wall of the elevator as it hummed steadily to the eighth floor. He fumbled momentarily with the key and stumbled inside. He automatically flipped on the TV but after a moment gave up any idea of watching it.

He worked his way unsteadily to the bedroom where he threw his clothes on a chair near the dresser. He wandered into the kitchen and back again with the screwdriver in his hand. He removed the letter from its place of concealment and read it once again.

"I'll be damned," he said.

He replaced the letter, fastened the cover, took two aspirins and crawled into bed.

Almost immediately he slipped into subconsciousness. It was not a restful sleep. His dreams were filled with nameless faces . . . with bodies riddled by schrapnel . . . with battlefields and screaming and men cursing and praying and dying.

He woke unexplainably before five o'clock, surprisingly sober and a little frightened. He lay there staring up at the ceiling until the sun had risen well into the sky before he was fortunate enough to drop back to sleep.

Chapter 3.

The next few days did not go by quickly. Mitchell plodded through the daily routine of an advertising agency account supervisor and realized more than ever that he'd been playing a role as long as he'd held the position. If he stayed at it another thirty years, would anyone recognize that point? He decided they probably wouldn't. Within the advertising community, he was considered uncommonly good at his job. When he'd first realized it a few years ago, it had come as a surprise to him.

There had been offers . . . several of them in fact. But Mitchell had turned everything down and his agency had gratefully taken this as an indication of his satisfaction with their organization. They gave him a substantial raise with each offer refusal and smugly told themselves that they indeed had more to offer than the other ad shops. In truth, Mitchell had never seriously considered another position because they offered nothing different from what he was already doing and he felt the changeover and the adjustment to a new operating procedure would be a pain in the butt he could do without.

Wednesday was a brilliant day, rarely perfect for so early in the spring. Mitchell was half way to the Loop before he decided to get off the bus and go home. He called in sick, and spent most of the day at Big Run Golf Club. He played unhurriedly, by himself, carding a seventy-eight, one of the best early season rounds he'd ever had.

It took an even greater effort than usual to force himself to work on Thursday. One of the agency's Vice-Presidents met him on the elevator.

"Hi, Dave. Missed you yesterday. How are you feeling?"

"Actually, I felt better yesterday."

"Maybe you tried to come back too soon."

"I think you're right."

"But I know you, Dave. Couldn't wait to get back to work."

The door opened at the eleventh floor and they both got off. "Yeah," Mitchell said. "You know me."

He answered letters, made phone calls, attended meetings, held appointments, made creative suggestions for two campaigns and finally, at four-thirty, left for home. Mitchell skipped his normal stop at the Boul Mich and took a cab rather than the bus that was his usual mode of transportation.

Nearly a week had gone by since he'd received the letter. The anticipation of hearing something further had grown steadily as the days passed.

Mitchell flipped the top of the metal mail box up and stared morosely at the empty interior. "Shit," he said, matter-of-factly.

He slammed the lid down and shaking his head, hit the elevator button to the eighth floor. Maybe there's been a change for some reason they aren't going to contact me, he thought. Day after tomorrow will be a whole week and the letter said. . . . Of course the whole damn thing could be some kind of practical joke . . . pretty elaborate, yet possible. He thought better of it. No . . . nobody he knew would have any reason. . . .

He was still deep in thought as he turned the key in the door, but it had only begun to swing open when he saw the envelope on the floor.

It was a plain, white, sealed envelope, with his name written across the front in firm, legible script. Mitchell closed the door and ripped open the letter.

A short note in the same distinct handwriting bore the date and said simply:

> Room 1710, Federal Building, Saturday, 7
> April 79, 0730 Hours. Enter through east
> side center door off Quincy Street.

There was a pass to the Federal Building enclosed in the envelope. The note wasn't signed.

Mitchell smiled broadly.

Chapter 4.

Seven-thirty in the morning is unreasonable for an appointment on any day. On Saturday it borders on the absurd.

A normal weekend might have found Dave Mitchell just getting to bed at this hour. But he'd curtailed his usual Friday night activities on this occasion and was atypically alert as he walked up the subway stairs on State Street. Inside he felt an increase in the building sense of excitement that had been growing for a week and was now reaching toward its culmination.

He'd wakened shortly after five o'clock, unable to sleep any longer, and left the house at five-thirty. At a pancake house on the near-north side, Mitchell had passed time with a large breakfast that was a rarity for him—bacon, eggs, hash-browns, milk and toast. He flipped through the paper with one eye on his watch.

Typically depressing news. The violent demonstrations were continuing in Germany. Israel and Egypt were both threatening one another. The Bulls were suffering through the worst season in their history. At seven o'clock he left to catch the subway to State and Adams.

There was an uncommon quiet in the middle of

Chicago's normally bustling Loop. It was one of the few times he'd seen the area when it wasn't amidst a great tumult. It was probably as near to restful as the core of that giant city can ever get.

Only two types of people were on the streets at this hour, those with a purpose and those who had lost all purpose. As he moved southward along State Street to Quincy, Mitchell wondered which group he fit into.

Quincy is a short dead end street that runs only a half block from State to the east side of the Federal Building. The main building entrances are on the southwest and northwest corners along Dearborn Street. Mitchell wondered if his instructions to use the east-center door might be in error when he tried the door and found it locked. He glanced at his watch. Seven-twenty-five. He rattled the door once more.

A businesslike young man in a security guard's uniform appeared suddenly and unlocked the door. Mitchell moved inside and fished in his pocket for the pass as the guard closed the door and crisply guided him away from it into a corridor between the two nearest elevator banks. As far as Mitchell could tell the building was deserted except for himself and the guard. He unfolded the pass and handed it across to the immaculately tailored young man who was eyeing him carefully.

"Not much business here on Saturday, I gather."

His attempt at conversation was ignored by the guard, who scarcely glanced at the pass. "Middle elevator bank," he said. Together, footsteps echoing loudly on the floor of the cavernous lobby, they walked to the center corridor of the building where the elevators that serviced the middle floors were located. The guard directed Mitchell into the elevator. "Room 1710 is on your left as you get off." The elevator doors closed.

Mitchell walked to his left down the hallway of the

seventeenth floor. Painted on the clear glass door of the third office from the end were the numerals "1710." He opened the door and went inside. It was a small reception room with one desk facing the door and several gray metal filing cabinets against the far wall. A window behind the desk overlooked Dearborn Street. Hanging on the wall beside the desk was an unimaginative painting of a flower arrangement. A brown leather couch and chair were at the right of the door. It was a plain room, very neat and workable, but drab. The reception area was empty and Mitchell looked curiously about and to the left of the desk through another door that opened into an adjoining office that was at least three times as large as the room he had entered. It was elegantly carpeted and more tastefully decorated than the outside room, but still a bit bleak.

The man in the huge chair behind the desk had been sitting so quietly that Mitchell hadn't noticed him and when he spoke it gave Mitchell a start.

"Come in, Mitchell," the man said. He stood and offered a firm hand. Mitchell was immediately struck by his stately appearance. "My name is Walker," the tall man said, "and I've got a lot I'd like to talk to you about. Have a seat."

Dave Mitchell took a seat in one of the two chairs that faced the desk. Frank Walker sat back and studied Mitchell silently for a few moments. Mitchell shifted his position and cleared his throat.

"What is it that you have in mind, Mr. Walker?"

"Call me Walker," he said, then added, "you're a little heavier than I'd imagined."

"Heavier?"

"Oh, nothing we can't correct—we'll fix that up in a hurry—just a little heavier than I thought you'd be." Walker raised himself fluidly from the swivel chair and walked to the side of the desk where he sat with one leg on the floor and the other dangling carelessly.

"Just give me a minute, Mitchell," he said. "You know how you form a mental picture of someone you've never seen?" He pulled a cigarette from his shirt pocket and offered one to Mitchell who declined it and lit one of his own. "Well, I'm just adjusting my mental picture to the real thing." He laughed easily as he lit the cigarette. "It's amazing how well I know you from our files, but the one thing we didn't have was a current picture." Walker slid off the edge of the desk and eased back into the swivel chair. "Every man is known for the things he does best, Mitchell; among my assets is supposedly the ability to judge character." He leaned forward in the chair and looked directly into Mitchell's eyes. "It's hard to judge character if you haven't actually seen a man's face, but I think I've been right about you. I think you'll work out just fine if you decide to get involved."

Mitchell wanted to get on with it. "Mr. Walker," he said, "I obviously have some interest in whatever it is that we're here for. I'd appreciate it if we could get into it."

Walker nodded. "You received a rather unusual letter last week, Mitchell. Right now you can't really appreciate the significance of it, but before you leave here this morning you will. I'm going to ask you some questions, give you a few facts and together we'll decide just how deeply you're going to get involved.

Walker unsnapped a briefcase on the floor beside his chair and tossed a manila folder on the desk top.

"You've been out of the army for four years now, Mitchell. How do you look at it in retrospect?"

Mitchell considered for a moment. "As some of the most significant years of my life," he said.

"If you felt that way about it, why did you get out?"

"I didn't feel that way about it at the time," Mitchell said. "When I got back from Vietnam I had a little sorting out to do. I thought I needed a change." He shrugged. "So I got out."

"Ever think about going back in?"

Mitchell liked the relaxed yet direct manner of this man and found his answers coming spontaneously. Some of them surprised him a bit because he hadn't consciously considered them before.

"Yes."

"How seriously?"

"The thought has crossed my mind a few times. Still, I've never thought about it seriously." He pondered it. "Maybe it's something I've held in the back of my mind . . . a trump card I could use if things got unbearable."

"And they apparently never got that bad?"

"I guess they haven't." He knit his brow as he tried to understand the way he really looked at it. "But no matter how tough things might get, I doubt that I'd ever admit I couldn't handle it."

"Not necessarily a bad trait," said Walker. "I suppose the ad agency business might be interesting."

Mitchell couldn't tell whether Walker was serious or not. "There are good points about it," he said.

"Captain, if you'll pardon me for saying so, I think it would bore the ass off a man who used to deal in matters of life and death." Walker pointed to the window. "There's a world out there where people live and die on their ability to make decisions and execute them. You've been inside that world. You've felt the pulse of it. . . ."

"And I've felt the pulse stop," Mitchell interrupted. "I've seen life end more times than a hundred average men."

"That's part of it," Walker said immediately. "And as you say, 'average' men." Walker pursued it enthusiastically. "You've experienced it, and you're the better for it. Was there ever a time, Captain, when you were more aware—sensed more, felt more, thought more—than those days when you knew death might be behind the next bush or in the next incoming round? Don't you believe that a man hasn't really lived if he's never gotten up in the morning and wondered if he'll live through the day?"

Mitchell thought this man, Walker, like all military men, was probably a little fanatical. He found it ironic that Walker had spoken the same thoughts that had run through his mind on occasion during the past four years.

He also became aware that he'd been addressed as "Captain." It had been a long time since that title had been used and Mitchell was flattered in spite of himself. It fit him well. He related with this extraordinary man who was suddenly making him wonder why he'd ever considered leaving the service. They both lit cigarettes.

"So, Mitchell," Walker continued, "what I have to determine today is whether or not you'd consider performing a mission for your country. Without exaggeration, I can say it's one of the most significant tasks that the intelligence community has ever been called on to perform."

He wanted to say yes unequivocally, but knew better. "You know I'd have to hear more before deciding."

"Of course you will," Walker said. "By the same token you realize I won't be able to go into complete specifics due to the nature of the project."

"Let's feel our way along then," Mitchell said.

Frank Walker agreed. Now that the preliminaries were over they both settled back further into their chairs and Walker began.

"I represent a rather select intelligence group, Mitchell. It's a small group; the exact number is classified. We have agents on assignment at various points throughout the world—anywhere the security of the United States or the free world might be threatened." Walker ran a hand absently through his thick graying hair and continued. "One of our men has been working in a country in Europe for several years. Recently he uncovered information that seems to be the most ominous news we've had in Europe since World War II."

Walker looked at Mitchell for a reaction but got none other than an expression that asked to be told more.

"We don't go off half-cocked, Mitchell," he said. "We're convinced this situation is absolutely critical. It requires some action to be taken." He paused for a moment and leaned forward over the desk. "That's where you come in."

Mitchell met his gaze evenly. "In what way?" he said.

"I can't be quite that specific now. But obviously we want you in on the mission."

Mitchell laughed a nervous sort of laugh. "Why me, Mr. Walker? I can't imagine any reason you'd come to me."

"I could give you a lot of reasons, but I won't just yet. Suffice it to say there are several unique requirements a participant in this mission has to have." Walker motioned nonchalantly toward Mitchell. "You fit them right down the line."

Mitchell was listening intently. "Go ahead."

"If you accept the mission, you'll be paid on a GS scale that's specially constructed for our unique little group. It's a hell of a lot of money, Mitchell . . . it requires a hell of a lot in return. I don't have to tell you our job isn't easy. People have been known to get killed in this line of work."

"What happens when the mission is over?"

"You're a permanent part of the group. You'll continue pulling the same salary between assignments as you do when you're working." Walker looked directly into Mitchell's eyes. "You should definitely understand one point—it's not an easy organization to get out of."

Mitchell understood.

"You might guess by the nature of our work we try to discourage a big turnover. Differs a little from the ad game in that respect."

Walker stroked the bridge of his nose absently with his forefinger. "I think we've arrived at the point now where you make your first decision. Do you want to get into more detail on this thing, or do you think you'd rather say good-bye now, walk out of here and forget it?"

Mitchell didn't hesitate with his reply. "I'd like to hear more."

Walker's features relaxed a bit as the answer he'd hoped for was given. "Well then, Mitchell, let's really get into it. I'll be as direct and detailed as possible under the circumstances. If you have questions, I'll answer them if I can."

Mitchell's stomach had tightened and his throat was dry. It reminded him of the feeling he used to get in high school before a football game. He was a little irritated that he wasn't able to control it. He hoped it wasn't noticeable.

"The country is Germany," Walker said. "You've probably read something about the unrest there in recent months."

The article he had read in the *Tribune* came to mind. "Yes, some quotes by the Chancellor last week. He played it down. There was more on it in this morning's paper".

"You probably also know this is unusual for that country . . . the reason for it is our problem." Walker took a deep breath and his tone changed slightly. Mitchell knew they were getting to the crux of the situation.

"There's a group within the country who's responsible for the unrest. They're using the theme of German unification and nationalism to build a base that will not only attempt to change the form of government in Germany but will attempt to shift the balance of power in Europe. If something isn't done to break this group up, they'll become the greatest military threat the free world has ever known!"

Mitchell laughed nervously and shook his head in disbelief. "Excuse me, sir," he said, "but this is a little bit of a mind blower. It's quite a lot to absorb."

Walker's features were set and deadly serious. "It was a lot for all of us to absorb. It may sound far-fetched, but believe me, it's genuine."

"How big a group is this?"

"Big enough to achieve their objective," Walker said. "As you know, numbers aren't always an accurate indicator of strength. We know the approximate number and just let it suffice to say they're big enough to achieve their objectives."

"And we stop them."

Walker nodded his head. "Right now, I can't give you the specifics of the mission . . . only that the successful completion of it will accomplish what we want." Walker picked up the folder from the desk and thumbed through it without really looking at it. "The mission will take place somewhere in Germany. We don't know exactly where as yet. It will take place as soon as we can train the participants . . . the sooner the better. At any rate, we feel it has to be done within a couple of months."

Mitchell registered surprise. "That doesn't seem like a

lot of time to get ready for something as important as you say this is."

"The fact that it *is* so important is why we're limited on time. We can't afford to put it off a day longer than we absolutely have to." Walker lit another cigarette and put the burned match in his pocket. "Don't worry," he said. "We'll have you ready for the mission. In fact, you might think you're over-trained."

"How many people will be involved?"

"Can't tell you that just now. That will come a little later. I *can* tell you that the training period will be highly concentrated and that we'll hold it in a remote area for security purposes."

They sat in silence for several minutes.

"Why doesn't the German government take care of it? Aren't we butting into something that might cause hard feelings?"

"They don't know about it," Walker said simply.

"Why don't we tell them?"

"You don't go to an ally and tell him that your intelligence network has uncovered something in his country that he's not aware of. I think you can see where they might not understand our need to have agents in their country in the first place. At best, it could hurt their feelings, and at worst, it could make them downright mad. In either case they'd probably ask us to get the hell out and we don't think that would be in our best interests."

The logic seemed obvious and Mitchell was a little embarrassed at raising the question. He went on to another. "There's something I have to ask again," he said. "Why me? You've got an organization of real pros . . . any number of them should be able to do whatever you need."

Walker nodded. "As I said, Mitchell, there are several

reasons . . . your security clearance . . . past military record . . . near perfect command of the German language . . . ability to pass for German in appearance . . . no family ties." Walker stopped. "Any problems there with your divorce and all?"

Mitchell shook his head. "My problems walked out three months ago."

Walker continued. "You're an expert with small arms weapons . . . military intelligence background . . . not currently in the military . . . liked the army . . . not completely satisfied with your present situation. . . ." Walker swiveled his chair to one side and rested an elbow on the table. "None of these things by themselves are particularly unusual, Mitchell. But put them all together and you cut the numbers who fill those criteria down considerably. Makes a fairly unique group."

Mitchell didn't completely understand. "Why is the fact I'm not in the Army important?"

"We don't want to take any chance that this organization knows we're on to them," Walker said. "You know how far dossier files go back. By using someone they have no records on, we're more likely to go unnoticed. As you said earlier, he continued, "we've got pros who could step in and do the job right now. We simply don't want to take the risk they'd be spotted and blow the whole mission. We've considered it all and think our best bet is men like yourself."

Mitchell needed a few moments to put everything into perspective. Walker was standing now and reminding Mitchell of the importance of the mission in preserving the democratic form of government in Europe. He also reminded him once again that it could be highly dangerous.

Walker checked his watch. "I think we've covered it, Mitchell." He thrust his arm out and firmly shook

Mitchell's hand. "You should have some time to think on this," he said. But obviously, we don't want to take too much. I'll call you tomorrow."

Before Mitchell knew it, he was in the hallway heading to the elevator. He marvelled at the enormity of it all. In the back of his consciousness he knew he'd made his decision and wondered why he hadn't told Walker outright. Oh, well, he told himself as the elevator stopped at the first floor, that might have been too hasty. They may not want a man who acts that impulsively.

Mitchell looked casually for the guard but didn't see him. The east-center door opened from the inside and locked behind him with a distinct click.

Back on the seventeenth floor of the Everett McKinley Dirksen Federal Building, Frank Walker, as per a routine that had developed over years of habit, methodically put the room back into its originally spotless condition, and locking the office door, strode whistling to a waiting elevator.

Chapter 5.

By eight-thirty in the morning, the sun had moved far enough across the sky that its rays were falling through the east windows of Dave Mitchell's apartment. The bedroom drapes were parted ever-so-slightly, allowing one penetrating thread of light to shoot into the room and fall exactly upon the sleeping left eye of the inert mass of flesh sprawled so ungracefully across the width of the bed. It danced back and forth across his face as a soft breeze stirred the drapes. Mitchell's eyelid twitched slightly in protest. After several minutes he turned over and reluctantly opened his eyes.

The memory of yesterday's meeting flooded back over him. The conversation had gone through his mind so often he was certain he could recite it verbatim.

He stretched and looked at his watch and tried to remember when he'd fallen asleep. The last thing he could recall was checking his watch at two-forty-five. He yawned and forced himself off the bed.

He had made the decision yesterday before he left the Federal Building. Now it was only a matter of waiting for Walker to call.

Mitchell had resigned himself to expecting the call late in the day and he was both surprised and relieved when the phone rang at ten o'clock. There was no mistaking the businesslike voice on the other end.

"Well, Captain?"

"Yes!" Mitchell said.

The relief at the other end of the line was apparent. "We've got some more things to discuss then—to get into the right atmosphere, how about lunch at the Black Forest? I understand that's a pretty respectable German restaurant and it's just a few blocks from you."

"Great. When should I meet you?"

"Twelve."

"See you then."

"See you then, Mitchell."

Mitchell strolled leisurely up Broadway. The street was busier than usual with a Sunday crowd browsing through shops or heading to the park. It was a minute before twelve when he walked through the door of the Black Forest.

The waiter promptly greeted him in German and showed him to a corner table where Frank Walker sat studying the wine list. He stood as Mitchell approached the table. They shook hands.

"Quite a selection," he motioned as they sat down.

"I haven't been here that often," Mitchell said, "but this place does have a good reputation."

"So I understand."

They sat there for an awkward moment and made inconsequential comments on the decor and the atmosphere. It was very much unlike both of them to do that. A striking blonde waitress brought their drinks.

Walker raised his glass to Mitchell. *"Prost."*

"Prost."

In only a few moments they had finished their drink and ordered a second.

"You know an awful lot about me, don't you, Walker?"

He nodded.

Mitchell pointed to his glass and spoke lightly, yet with seriousness at the same time. "And the fact I've got a great fondness for liquor doesn't count against me?"

Walker was well into his second drink. "You may have noticed that I occasionally imbibe myself." He rearranged the silverware in front of him. "I won't say we didn't take a hard look at that particular point," he said. "But we don't have any reason to think you can't handle it. And besides, Mitchell," he added, "we think you'll probably have enough sense to use a little restraint when the situation requires it." He threw off the rest of the glass and motioned to the waiters. "But as for now, we might as well celebrate."

He ordered another round.

Mitchell thought he'd probably get to like Walker.

"I guess there are a few things we should cover before we get totally wasted," Walker said.

Mitchell moved his chair closer to the table and rested his elbows on it. Walker went on.

"Can you be ready to leave here next weekend?"

"For good?"

"Lock, stock and barrel."

"I guess so."

"You can do it anyway you want, but I'd suggest you get pissed off about something at work and just walk out."

Mitchell couldn't help smiling. It wasn't a new idea for him.

"It has to be something abrupt because we don't have time to waste." Walker had finished another drink and Mitchell found himself in the unusual situation of trying to catch up. "At the same time," Walker continued, "what you do has to be consistent with your character. It can't be so unusual that no one can understand your doing it."

"We don't have to worry about that. I can come up with something."

"Good," Walker said. "Nothing to hold you here?"

Mitchell thought. "No . . . well . . . maybe a problem with the apartment. . . ."

"Get rid of it. If it costs you anything, we'll pick it up."

". . . nothing else I can think of."

"No girls?"

"I know a few—but none I have to answer to."

They ordered dinner and another round of drinks. Both of them were beginning to feel the effects but neither allowed themselves to show it. Walker went on.

"Tell everyone you don't have any plans, you're just taking off. Pack what you want in your car and sell the rest. Again, we'll pay for any loss you have to take." Walker pulled an envelope from inside his jacket pocket. "Ever been to Colorado?"

"Matter-of-fact I've spent a lot of time there . . . between Denver and the University of Colorado."

"Well, don't look up any old friends." He pushed the envelope across the table. "This is a hotel reservation for you in Boulder. For next Thursday."

"Why Thursday? Do I have to be there that soon?"

"No significance in the day. The reservation runs through the following week. That should give you plenty of time to tie up any loose ends you have here. But we want you out there as soon as possible." Walker thought a moment and lit a cigarette. "As I said, we want you to drive. We'll take care of your car later."

"What happens when I get there?"

"You'll be contacted. Like I said yesterday, I won't be

able to tell you everything about the mission at once. For security reasons, you'll get it piecemeal." Their food arrived and Walker continued as they ate. "For now just let me say that your training will start as soon as possible after you get there."

"Will we be training in Colorado?"

"We'll be in Colorado."

"How long will the training take?"

"We hope it doesn't last too long, but it'll last as long as necessary." Walker motioned about the room. "I said on the phone today that I thought this would be a good place to set the mood for what's coming up."

Mitchell nodded.

"One of the primary objectives of the training is to pass you off as German. You'll speak German, eat German, refresh your memory as to their customs—anything that will help you fit into their contemporary scene without drawing attention to yourself."

"What kind of cover will I have?"

"You'll have suitable cover. We'll give you specifics in due time."

They finished their meals and both refused dessert. Walker was leaning back in his chair and eyeing the waitresses. "Say, Mitchell," he said abruptly, "may I ask you what you did with the letter you got that first started this whole thing?"

Mitchell was surprised and a little embarrassed. "Well," he said, "I still have it."

"Really?" Walker said. "You don't carry it on you?"

"No," Mitchell said. "I—it's hidden."

"In your apartment?"

"Yes."

Walker smiled broadly, then chuckled aloud.

"What's so funny?"

"Not really funny," Walker apologized. "I guess you

might say I'm pleased."

Mitchell's expression asked for an explanation.

"I hope you won't mind this Mitchell, but you understand that while I had a great file on you, it was necessary to look through your quarters too."

"What!"

"You can get a lot of clues about a man's character by going through his dresser drawers," Walker said.

"You had someone go through my apartment?"

"Oh, no, Mitchell. I'd never leave something that important to someone else. I went through it myself."

"Where the hell do you. . ."

Walker interrupted. "Now, Captain, you're missing the point here. You know it was necessary . . . and you obviously passed the inspection." Walker smiled again. "But the thing that really interests me is the letter. You know, I felt you'd have a tendency to keep it. And since it is rather sensitive, I thought I'd play a little game and look for it." He raised an empty glass to Mitchell. "Congratulations. I couldn't find it."

The fact someone had gone through his apartment didn't bother Mitchell as much as the fact that he hadn't noticed any indication of it. At the same time he was silently gloating that Walker hadn't found the letter.

"At any rate," Walker said, "burn the letter."

"All right," Mitchell said.

Walker fidgeted a bit and Mitchell sensed his discomfort at something he was about to say.

"Mitchell," Walker said at last, "where *did* you hide the damn thing?"

Mitchell laughed. "Walker, there'll be damn few times I'm one up on you—I'm going to hang on to this one."

Walker shrugged it off. "You know what, Captain? I think we've just about covered it. Now we can get down to some serious drinking."

This is a man after my own heart, thought Mitchell.

It was nearly five o'clock when they stumbled out the front door onto Clark Street.

Mitchell walked north to Diversey and then east to Lincoln Park. It had been enjoyable. He'd learned as much as he could expect. Walker seemed straight, someone that Mitchell could level with.

There had been one question though, a question that had passed through his mind several times during the afternoon. He hadn't asked it because he knew it wasn't applicable.

But as he walked along the edge of Lincoln Park now, he wondered again what would have happened if he had decided *not* to accept the mission in the first place? Or even more interesting, what if he decided now that he didn't want to take part? What would Walker do then? He shivered slightly and pulled his jacket collar up firmly about his neck. Must be a chill coming off the lake, he thought.

Chapter 6.

Rain began falling late Sunday night in Chicago and a heavy overcast and intermittent drizzle continued to mid-morning the next day. From indications, it appeared to be one of those steady, monotonous spring rain storms that come up on the gulf stream and get locked over the city when the winds off Lake Michigan neutralize it. It was the kind of weather that might easily last for several days and had a generally depressing effect.

Monday morning was business as usual at Jackman, Ryder & Hutchins. The adverse weather had scarcely been noticed by Dave Mitchell. He reported to work with an abnormal enthusiasm for a Monday morning and later reminded himself to suppress it lest someone suspect something out of the ordinary was in the offing. Most of the morning was spent considering various situations to use as an excuse for leaving. By noon, he hadn't come up with an appropriate solution, but when he returned from lunch his secretary was waving a message to catch his eye.

"Mr. Nesselson called while you were out."

"Dammit, what a shame I missed him." Mitchell's sarcasm left little doubt about the feelings he held for his caller. "What did he want?"

"Didn't say . . . as soon as he found out you weren't in, he asked for Ron Stevens . . . then a few minutes later Ron rang back and told me to have you call as soon as you got in."

In addition to being the most obnoxious person Mitchell had ever met, Nesselson also happened to be in charge of new products research for Midwest Foods, Jackman, Ryder & Hutchins' largest account. In the excitement of the last few days Mitchell had nearly forgotten the campaign he had put together to promote Midwest's latest product line, an entry into the frozen food market. A meeting with Nesselson was normally the last thing in the world Mitchell wanted but he found himself smiling sardonically now as he contemplated an appointment which he felt certain would provide the appropriate setting for his exit from Jackman, Ryder & Hutchins. His secretary interrupted his thoughts.

"Ron said it was urgent."

Gaunt, bespectacled Ron Stevens was the management supervisor for Jackman, Ryder & Hutchins. As the account supervisor, Mitchell had three account executives under him while reporting directly to Stevens. They worked well together, Mitchell and Stevens, despite the fact Stevens worried about things too much. That particular trait was not one that Mitchell shared. "That sort of seriousness," Mitchell had once told Stevens, "is only appropriate in two places—in bed or on a golf course." Nevertheless, he liked Stevens more than he liked anyone else at Jackman, Ryder & Hutchins.

On the other hand, Stevens knew he had an unusual talent in Mitchell. He'd taken care of him because the good work Mitchell had done created enough glory for both of them to bask in. Stevens and Mitchell both knew Mitchell could take over Stevens' job if he really had a mind to, and as long as Mitchell was content with the status quo, Stevens wasn't about to make waves.

The phone rang only once before it was picked up at the other end. "Stevens here."

"This is Dave, Ron."

"Oh, Dave, I'm glad you called." Mitchell could hear a frantic shuffling of papers through the receiver as the voice on the line raced on. "Nesselson called today. Pissed off because you weren't here."

"Screw him. What the hell does he expect me to do, sit here through lunch hour in case he calls?"

Stevens knew enough not to argue about it. "He's ready to hear our pitch on the new frozen food dinners. Everything set?"

"Set."

"What have you got?"

"Everything we need. Budget's set . . . sample ads . . . campaign philosophy . . . timing . . . target audience. . . ."

"Is it all put together? Can we pitch it tomorrow?"

Mitchell smiled broadly. "Tomorrow sounds perfect to me. The sooner, the better."

"I've never heard you so anxious to see Nesselson."

"The sooner we get it over with, the better."

"So you'll have it all together?"

"Jerry and I will go through things one final time to double check, but we're OK. Our place or his?"

"His. I think just you, I and Jerry will go. No need for anybody else that I can see."

"Right." Mitchell checked his watch. "Listen, I'd better get to work. What time tomorrow?"

"Ten o'clock. We'll leave at nine-thirty."

"Call you later."

Mitchell replaced the receiver in its cradle and leaned back in his chair. He hadn't expected Nesselson to ask for the Midwest campaign plans this quickly, but now that it had happened, it was perfect. Mitchell had set up a good campaign, well-planned and prepared. Anyone who saw the plans would have to be favorably impressed. Mitchell corrected himself. That is, anyone except Nesselson.

He spent the rest of the afternoon tying up loose ends and putting the final touches on the presentation. At four-thirty he called in Ron Stevens and together they went through it.

"Good job," Stevens said as Mitchell finished. "I've got a feeling tomorrow's going to be an important day for us."

Mitchell nodded vaguely as he replaced art boards in their proper sequence. "Should be a day to remember, all right."

Shortly after nine-thirty the next morning, a group of typical Chicago admen emerged from the offices of Jackman, Ryder & Hutchins, bearing the various paraphernalia that identified their trade. In a matter of seconds they had hailed a cab on Michigan Avenue and loaded into it two extremely cumbersome and awkward art portfolios, a slide projector and one casette tape recorder.

Stan Ryder, the "Ryder" of Jackman, Ryder & Hutchins, was an unscheduled late starter in what was now a foursome. Mitchell regarded this last minute addition as advantageous. As the cab wound its way through the morning traffic to Chicago's northwest side, Mitchell made it a point to mention the thought and effort that had been put into the campaign. It was important that he convince Stan Ryder that the presentation was something he had become very much involved in. Still, he couldn't risk over-playing it. Contrary to several individuals Mitchell could think of, Stan Ryder hadn't arrived at his current station in life through any circumstance other than hard work. Consequently, he wasn't the type who allowed much to slip by.

Ron Stevens, as was his habit, talked aimlessly and incessantly all the way to the account and it was with no small sense of relief that the other three departed the cab and entered the reception room of Midwest Foods. In a matter of moments they were ushered through a winding maze of offices and cubicles into the spacious walnut paneled conference room that occupied the northwest corner of the sprawling first floor. A huge, elongated mahogany table flanked on each of its two long sides by ten chairs, occupied the center of the room. Spaced evenly at intervals atop the table were pitchers of ice water, each surrounded by several glasses, resting on cork-lined metal serving trays. A projector stand was positioned at one end of the table, and on the wall opposite it, a portable easel and an attached movie screen which rolled up into its case when not in use. On the side wall above the table, the portrait of the founder of Midwest Foods stared sternly down on the room.

They arranged and double-checked their equipment and waited for nearly ten minutes before a fat, balding man of fifty entered the room, followed dutifully by two younger men whose actions identified them as subordinates. Nesselson greeted everyone in his perfunctory manner and took a seat near the middle of the table. His glasses sat low on the nose of a reddish face and his eyes were large and wide. When he spoke it was in a fast high pitched voice that sounded as if it were on the verge of hysteria.

"Glad to see you here today, Stan," he said. "Who's giving the show?"

Mitchell thought if frogs were red, Nesselson would look exactly like one.

Stan Ryder nodded toward Mitchell. "Dave Mitchell's been our primary man on this project, backed up our course by Ron Stevens. Mitchell's going to handle the presentation, and gentlemen, if you're ready I'll ask Dave to take it away."

Nesselson grunted.

"Gentlemen," said Mitchell as the first pictures flashed upon the screen, "may we present 'Midwest's Best,' a new line of frozen food products."

The product name was presented; the packaging; sample print, radio and TV ads; introductory campaign schedule and the breakdown of the first year's proposed budget.

The presentation was nearly perfect. In fact as he wrapped up the summary thirty minutes later, Mitchell began to worry that Nesselson might break a long-standing tradition and accept the idea exactly as presented.

The lights came up and Mitchell switched off the lamp of the projector. "Well, Mr. Nesselson, how does it sound to you?"

Nesselson puffed seriously on the cigar clamped between his teeth. It was a moment before he answered.

"I don't like it."

"Why not?" Mitchell asked. "Those sample ads are as good as any you'll ever see."

He left the cigar in his mouth and the end bobbed up and down as he talked. "I don't like the name. The packaging's OK, the ad copy and creative is OK, the budget's OK . . . it's just the name."

Mitchell knew he must pursue this aggressively. He made certain his tone conveyed his feelings. "How can you say the copy and creative is OK and the name isn't? The copy and creative is hinged on the product name. If you don't have the name, those ads aren't worth a damn."

Nesselson wasn't one to be lectured. And certainly not on his home turf. "Well, if you put it that way, it's not worth a damn!"

Stan Ryder knew Nesselson well enough to know they could probably get around this if they used a little tact. "A lot of thought went into this, Ed."

"It just seems to me like it isn't very creative, Stan. We don't come out with a new product line very often. Frankly, I'd hoped for better."

Mitchell tried to fan the fire up again.

"Well, I'll agree it's not the most exotic name in the world, but then again, how exotic are frozen foods?"

"Goddammit, Mitchell, if there isn't a better name than 'Midwest's Best,' I don't know anything about the food business!"

"That's a possibility you might consider," Mitchell shot back.

Nesselson's face was beginning its change from darkening shades of pink to what would ultimately become a deep crimson in color. "Well I'm damned sure that if I called myself a creative person, as I assume you do, I'd come up with a name that would stir up a little *excitement,* a little *stimulation!"* he screeched.

Stan Ryder made an effort to tone things down, but the situation had already gotten out of control. Ron Stevens sat the end of the table and viewed the proceedings as if watching a bad dream. Now it was Mitchell coming back at Nesselson.

"What do you think we're naming . . . a whorehouse? We're talking about frozen food products here, nothing more! We've picked a simple effective name that fits the product. A lot of people who know what they're doing decided on it. Frankly, I don't think you know more than that group!"

"Well, I'll tell you something, Mitchell, and you listen real good!" Nesselson waved a pudgy finger in Mitchell's direction and with each sentence, the volume and pitch of his voice went up. "We're not using the name—period! If you can't come up with a better one, we won't use you—period!" He grabbed the cigar from his mouth and used it to point for emphasis. "In the meantime, I've got a warehouse full of frozen food; now what the hell am I supposed to do with that?"

A smile uncontrollably flickered across Mitchell's face.

"Well, Mitchell?" Nesselson screamed. "Do you hear me? Just what the hell am I going to do with a warehouse full of frozen food?"

Mitchell told him.

It was a quiet ride back to the Loop. Stan Ryder had done the only thing he could, that being to tell Mitchell in Ed Nesselson's presence, that he was off the Midwest Foods account. He'd apologized to Nesselson saying that Mitchell had been so personally involved in the campaign that he'd been a little sensitive about it. Nesselson considered that a rather gross understatement. A promise was made to review the campaign and come up with an alternate proposal.

Stan Ryder didn't want to lose Dave Mitchell and offered him another account responsibility after they returned to the office. But Mitchell, after apologizing for his behavior, explained that he felt he should take some time off to unwind a bit. Later that afternoon, he turned in his resignation, which, despite the rather unpleasant activities of the day, was accepted with great reluctance. By four that afternoon he had cleaned out his desk and left Jackman, Ryder & Hutchins for the last time.

Within three days he had sold all but his essential belongings and was speeding across the rolling plains of Nebraska toward Boulder, Colorado.

Chapter 7.

The Rocky Mountains rise up abruptly a short distance west of Denver. Rather than beginning gradually and increasing in elevation over a period of miles, foothills are nearly nonexistent. Rolling grassy plains give way suddenly to gigantic masses of granite thrust upward from the earth's surface. At the base of these imposing phenomena, in one of the beautiful settings in the country, lies Boulder, Colorado.

He had made good time since leaving Omaha that morning, and had swung slightly out of his way to pass through Denver. He navigated Denver without a flaw, taking the Valley Highway to the Denver-Boulder Turnpike and then west to Boulder. Once in Boulder, he turned off Twenty-Eighth Street as the Master Hosts Motor Hotel came into view on his left. He parked near the main entrance.

The desk clerk recognized his name. "Ah, yes, Mr. Mitchell. We've been expecting you. I have something here for you." He reached under the counter and produced a thick brown business envelope. There was no marking on it other than Mitchell's name.

A bellhop showed Mitchell to his room on the fourteenth floor. He snapped open the drapes and the Rocky

Mountains burst again into view, the huge window framing their rugged countenance in a larger-than-life picture. On the left the three smooth, oddly shaped giant slabs, aptly named "Flatirons," rose above the south-west portion of Boulder.

Mitchell stood a moment and let the scene settle itself on his mind. It was something unique. No matter how many times he'd seen it, it never failed to stir his emotions.

The bellhop shifted his weight uncomfortably and cleared his throat. "Will there be anything else, sir?"

Mitchell snapped back to awareness. He tipped the bellhop and asked for a cold six-pack of Coors to be sent up.

Mitchell's room was large, essentially decorated in the same scheme as the downstairs lobby with the exception that his furniture, rug and bedspread were a deep brilliant yellow rather than the red which complemented the lobby and hallways. A king-size bed was against the left wall, with a larger-than-standard-size motel desk and dresser combination against the opposite wall. A Tiffany lamp hung from the ceiling in the corner near the window and under it, a circular table and two comfortable-looking yellow upholstered chairs. The bath and shower were modern, and substantially larger than most. He nodded in approval.

He still held the envelope that the desk clerk had given him and he opened it now and removed the contents. There were fifteen twenty dollar bills and a handwritten note. The note read:

> Welcome to Colorful Colorado. Here's
> something to help tide you over.
> You'll be contacted.

There was no signature.

Mitchell counted the money. Three hundred dollars.

There was a knock on the door and the bellhop came in with a large ice bucket containing six cans of Coors beer. "Made with pure Rocky Mountain spring water," he announced.

Mitchell paid him and tipped him and the bellhop left.

Mitchell turned the light out and faced one of the yellow upholstered chairs toward the window. He put the ice bucket on the table, eased himself into the chair, propped his feet up on the air conditioning unit and opened a beer.

It was very cold and beads of moisture formed on the can in his hand. He thought back to when he had last been in Colorado. It had been five years. He went to college at a small teacher's college in western Kansas. It was from that point that he and two friends had set out on many memorable and infamous weekends in Denver and Boulder.

He rested his head against the back of the chair and smiled as he relived some of the more outrageous incidents of those past years.

Outside the sun had disappeared behind the mass of the mountains, silhouetting their rugged black features against a fading red sky.

Mitchell suddenly realized how tired he was. He stretched luxuriously in the chair and allowed the tiredness that had been creeping slowly through his body, to engulf him.

He drained the beer, then picked up the phone and called the desk. It was eight o'clock. Through the windows, lights from the University shone in the distance.

"Desk."

"Room 1460. Call me in two and a half hours, please, at ten-thirty."

"Yes, sir."

He hung up the phone and kicked off his shoes and

lay back on the bed.

It seemed as if only five minutes passed before the phone rang, but when he finally managed to grasp the receiver and grunted into it, the desk clerk informed him that it was ten-thirty. Mitchell fought with himself for several minutes and very nearly ended up rolling back over and falling asleep again.

"What the hell," he said aloud, forcing himself to his feet. "I can sleep when I'm an old man."

Mitchell drove to a familiar area of Boulder known as "The Hill." To his disappointment, the long, narrow neon sign that used to read "Tulagi," was not to be seen. The building was still there, and judging by the size of the crowd outside, it was still a popular watering hole. Mitchell parked a few blocks away and walked back.

Inside, it had changed very little. The faces of the shoulder to shoulder crowd that jammed the bar area were different, the dress modified somewhat, but the people were the same.

Mitchell got a beer and worked his way further through the throng, beyond the bar where the room widened dramatically into a huge dance floor flanked with several rows of tables against the walls on both sides. From the far end of the floor, the bank belted out their music from atop a raised stage. He stood near a table at the right of the dance floor and watched and drank.

Three hours later, Mitchell left with an attractive graduate student in Geology with whom he'd spent most of the evening. When he finally left her apartment the sun had risen in the east and illuminated the highest peaks of the Rockies. As Mitchell stepped out into the cool mountain air, he concluded with absolute certainty that his friend had not devoted all her time to the research of Geology.

Mitchell spent the next day fishing the Big Thompson River in nearby Loveland.

It was nine o'clock when he returned to Boulder.

"Anything for 1460?" he asked at the desk.

The clerk produced two things from the message box. The first was a hand-written envelope similar in appearance to the one Mitchell received when he checked in. The other item was a note to the clerk which he read while handing Mitchell the first envelope.

"Seems we have a package for you, sir. If you'll bear with me a moment. . . ."

Mitchell nodded and the clerk excused himself and went into the office at the right-rear of the desk area. He emerged a moment later, struggling slightly with a bulky one-and-a-half by four foot cardboard box.

"Here you are, sir." He looked about for one of the bellhops. I'll get one of our young men to give you a hand."

"I can handle it," Mitchell said, hoisting the box onto his right shoulder.

"It's no trouble, sir. . . ."

"Thanks anyway."

Upstairs, he unlocked the door to his room, switched on the lights and threw the box on top of the bed. He ripped open the envelope and read the note.

> Check out Monday at 1600 Hours. Take your belongings and the contents of this box. Get in your car and drive west out of Boulder on Highway 119. Exactly five miles from the edge of the city limits, you'll see a hitchhiker with an Army fatigue jacket and a pack exactly like yours. Pick him up.

Mitchell read the note again, then tore it up and flushed it down the toilet. He ripped open the box and examined the sturdy back pack that was inside. A quick inspection indicated it was expertly packed and Mitchell decided not to succumb to his curiosity and drag everything out. Whoever had sent it looked like he knew what he was doing. Also in the box was a pair of black combat boots, a change of casual outdoor clothing, all in his size, and a sleeping bag. He smiled in admiration of someone's thoroughness as he put the pack and other articles in the alcove near the door.

He walked to the window and opened the drapes. The black mass of the mountains was scarcely definable against the sky. He stared into the darkness for several minutes, wondering what the next few days would bring.

At four-fifteen on Monday, as Mitchell rounded a sharp curve in the road, the familiar figure of a man in an O.D. jacket came into view. He carried two packs that matched the one Mitchell had earlier loaded in the back seat.

Walker didn't look up until Mitchell pulled alongside him. He unhooked the packs, and lowered them to the floor of the back seat. Then he eased his long frame into the car.

"*Guten Tag*, Captain," he said.

"Hello, Walker."

"We have quite a distance left," Walker said, motioning down the road. "We might as well get started."

Mitchell put the car in gear. Ahead of them, the sun was sinking gradually lower in the west. He pulled back onto the road and they drove into the sun, climbing steadily higher into the forested mountains.

Chapter 8.

"Did everything work out all right in Chicago?"

Mitchell recounted the events leading up to his departure. It gave him a feeling of satisfaction to think of it again.

Walker nodded in approval. He glanced into the back seat. "I see you got all your deliveries."

"Including the envelope full of twenties. Thanks particularly for that."

Walker brushed it off. "You'll be well taken care of." His voice trailed off and he stared out the window at the passing magnificence of their surroundings.

Mitchell glanced over at his passenger as he drove. The shadows and sunlight in turn skipped from behind tall pine and rock formations and danced across the august face that peered seriously back at them. He looked, Mitchell thought, even more impressive than he had remembered him. His face appeared more deeply tanned than it had back in Chicago. Now, as he studied him in the gathering twilight, Mitchell felt that Walker was one of those rare military commanders who could spur men to life and death action by his mere presence. Many commanders can compel action; very few can inspire it. Walker, he decided, was one of the very few.

They traveled in silence for some time. Walker finally spoke.

"Beautiful, isn't it?" He drew his attention back from the outside and looked at Mitchell. "But I'm sure you have more than the scenery on your mind."

"You could say I've got a question or two."

"Let me give you a few more facts. Then I'll answer what questions I can." Walker took a pack of cigarettes from his jacket pocket, lit one, and threw the pack on the dashboard. "To begin with, as of now, your name is Eric Werner. That's what you'll be called from this point until the completion of the mission. You'll react to that name as your own. You'll forget you ever knew anyone called Mitchell."

"And what kind of person will Eric Werner be?"

"Eric Werner is a bright young businessman from Stuttgart, Germany. He'll be returning to Stuttgart sometime within the next month from a business trip in the U.S.—"

"You said some time within a month. What determines the exact timing?"

"The first thing is how long it takes you to get ready. The second is to wait for the right moment."

"And what determines that?"

"I'll let you in on that at a later date." His tone indicated it would be fruitless to pursue the point.

"And the mission takes place in Stuttgart?"

"No, Stuttgart will be used only as a home of record for Werner . . . a place to clear customs from the U.S. From there, you'll travel to your destination as an average German businessman on a routine trip."

Ahead, in the fading light and long shadows at the side of the road, a grazing deer started at the sound of the approaching vehicle and bounded gracefully into the gathering darkness of the forest. Walker's eyes systematically searched the thicket as they drove past.

"Another thing that takes place beginning right now . . . to help you get set for your role as a German national, we'll speak nothing but German. No exceptions. Understood?"

"*Ich verstehe*," said Mitchell.

They made small talk in German and Mitchell was pleased with how well he had retained command of the language. They talked for nearly a half hour and then drove along in silence.

It was a winding mountain road and even though they seldom met other cars, Mitchell rarely exceeded fifty miles an hour. They drove steadily higher and as darkness was settling around them, they passed a sign indicating they had just crossed the Continental Divide.

"It's all downhill from here," Walker remarked dryly.

Another half hour passed before Walker stirred and leaned forward on the seat and peered intently out the window to the front. Ahead of them a luminous highway sign came into view.

"*Nach links*," he said.

The sign read, "Blue Mountain Reservoir—3 miles." Mitchell turned left onto the gravel road as Walker had instructed him. Shortly they arrived at a crossroad that branched and then circled the lake. They followed the portion of the road that went straight ahead for nearly a mile and then wound its way over the cliffs above the west shoreline. They were approaching the area along the western bank where the road reached its highest point above the surface level of the lake below.

"Pull in here." Walker indicated a small area between two stands of trees at the right side of the road.

Mitchell pulled off the road and the headlights of the car swept out across the edge of the cliffs and into the blackness beyond. The ground sloped gently from where they stopped to the cliff's edge, some thirty feet away. From there, it fell off into a sheer vertical drop of fifty feet.

"Put on the emergency," Walker said.

While Mitchell engaged the brake, Walker was lifting the three packs over the back seat into the front.

"We're going to ditch the car here," Walker said. "Just a little insurance move." Walker dropped two of the packs out the window and opened the third. "We'll let the car go over the cliff with this inside." He showed Mitchell the contents of the third pack. It matched the one which had been delivered to him two days earlier in Boulder.

"What if someone's seen the lights?"

"I'm sure they have. We want them to, just to make certain our efforts don't go unnoticed," Walker said. "What we *don't* want is for them to know you got out." Walker pulled a bottle of bourbon from the pack. "We'll go out the window, so the roof light won't go on."

Mitchell went through feet first and Walker followed him. It was a dark night and the moonlight was partially obscured by scattered clouds. It was almost nine o'clock.

Walker unscrewed the cap and threw the bottle on the floor of the front seat.

"Get our packs and take them back behind the trees."

Mitchell moved the packs and Walker broke a sturdy four-foot branch from a tree near the roadside. He signaled Mitchell to stay behind the trees and returned to the car. Reaching through the window, Walker pressed the branch firmly upon the foot brake. With his left hand, he released the emergency and then nudged the automatic gearshift. The car jerked as the transmission engaged, but the steady pressure of the branch on the brake held it in position. Then in one quick motion, Walker lifted the branch off the brake and jammed it onto the accelerator. The car lurched ahead with a roar, spinning earth behind it. Walker took two quick steps forward and then lowered himself to the ground.

The car plunged off the steep embankment, hurtled through the air for a few brief seconds, and dived nose-first with a great splash into the icy black water. The motor sputtered and stopped. It sank almost immediately.

From several hundred yards down the bank to the left a shout split the air, then several voices followed in shock and urgency. The commotion echoed off the surface of the water and bounced off the rock cliffs and rose in the thin air.

Walker withdrew quickly but stealthily. He grabbed his pack and attached it on his back. Mitchell likewise threw his pack over his shoulders and secured it.

"It will be morning before they get someone up here to pull the car out," Walker whispered. "It won't take them long to trace the registration. They'll find a pack, and an empty bourbon bottle. They'll either think you drove in on purpose or had one too many and went off the road." Walker had pulled out a military compass with a luminous dial and was engaged in shooting an azimuth. "At any rate, you got out of the car, but apparently couldn't get to shore . . . missing and presumed drowned."

Walker looked up from his compass and sighted a line on the top of an uneven ridge that crossed perpendicularly to them several hundred yards away.

"I've got our first point fixed. We'd better be moving out. We've got an appointment four miles from here at exactly 2400 Hours."

Together they crossed the road and Walker scrambled up the far bank and into the forest with Mitchell close behind.

It was harsh, thickly forested terrain and not easy to navigate in the dark, but Walker moved on purposefully, stopping only to check his compass and fix new reference points.

They hadn't been talking much since leaving the lake, mainly because their attention was taken up by the task at hand. Only once had Mitchell forgotten his instruction to use only the German language and Walker had quickly corrected him.

It was nearly two hours since they had left the lake and they were stopped now on a wooded knoll that overlooked a small valley. The clouds had slipped away and the moon had risen higher. A myriad of stars filled the sky. The moonlight glimmered on a stream that wound through the valley below. In the distance a night bird called and then it was silent, save for the heavy breathing of Mitchell.

"Where are we headed?"

Walker rechecked his compass reading and pointed over the nearby ridge on the far side of the valley. "We're eventually going to end up in the most remote and uninhabited part of the Rocky Mountains that we could find."

"And that's where we'll train?"

"Right . . . no fear of interruptions . . . no questions about what we're up to. . . ."

"Isn't there always a chance some real outdoors freak could stumble onto us?"

"There's a chance, but it's awfully slim. We've checked the area pretty thoroughly. It's about as secure as any place we could go."

"Why not a military fort?"

"Too many people have to know what you're doing there." He shook his head in confirmation. "No, this is the only way . . . just you and me."

Mitchell was a little surprised. He had expected to meet the others involved in the mission. "Won't there be anyone else there?"

"Just us."

Mitchell was breathing easier now after the short rest. "How far are we going?"

Walker was moving again. "Just over this ridge for now."

They moved down into the valley and after a short surveillance found a shallow spot to ford the fast running stream. The mountain water ran over and into Mitchell's boots and was cold and refreshing on his feet. They made their way quickly up the ridge on the other side. Across the ridge, there was a clearing in the pines that ran for some thirty meters before falling off into a ravine that eventually worked its way down to join with the valley they had just crossed.

Walker checked his watch. "2345 Hours," he said. His voice had a tinge of disappointment in it. "I thought we'd be here around 2300 Hours even."

"Well, we had to get here by 2400 and we made it," Mitchell said. "It wasn't exactly easy covering that terrain in the dark."

Walker grunted. He sat down near the edge of the clearing and lit a cigarette. Mitchell did the same. From below, the sound of the steadily falling stream gurgling across its rocky bed was the only sound to be heard. They sat there in the dark and smoked.

It was exactly fifteen minutes later when another familiar sound came to Mitchell's ears, faintly at first, gradually increasing in volume to overcome the sound of the stream as the "whop-whop-whop" of rotor blades slapping the air echoed in the mountains.

Walker scrambled to his feet and grabbed a flashlight from his pack. Momentarily the helicopter appeared and Walker pointed the beam skyward and began to systematically flash it. A return flash from the helicopter acknowledged his location. Within a minute the Army HU1E had set down in the clearing.

They ran, crouched over, to the helicopter. Mitchell

felt the wind, whipped by the rotors, in his face and a familiar thrill stirred in his stomach and rose into his chest as he ran and jumped through the open side door as he had done so many times before. He half expected to hear the whining of enemy bullets zipping overhead. The helicopter lifted off and it was some time before the exhilaration abated.

"Like old times," he laughed.

Walker laughed himself and slapped Mitchell on the back and for some reason they were both laughing uncontrollably as the helicopter headed toward the southeast.

In a half hour they touched down at another small clearing, many miles further into the mountains. During the flight the only evidence of life Mitchell had seen were the lights from one isolated ranch and that, over twenty minutes ago.

They jumped out and ran clear of the whirling blades and Walker motioned to the pilot. He lifted off and disappeared into the mountains behind them.

"Well, Eric," Walker said, "we've just covered ground in the last half hour that it would have taken us days to walk."

Mitchell motioned about them. "Is this it then?"

"No . . . we've still got several miles to go, but the terrain is too rough for a helicopter landing.

The mountain air was very chilly now. The soft pine needles on the forest floor made a comfortable walking surface and their aroma, mixed with the rich smell of the earth and the clean mountain air, filled his nostrils. They went on another fifteen minutes to a small level area atop a tree covered ridge.

"We'll camp here," said Walker.

Chapter 9.

It was shortly after five-thirty when Mitchell blinked the sleep from his eyes. A fine gray mist was settled along the ridge and obscured the trees beyond. The valley below was shrouded in thick fog.

He lay there for several minutes peering into the moist veil that engulfed them. There was scarcely a breath of wind and small particles of moisture hung suspended in the air. The presence of the fog accented the almost absolute silence. The absence of sound, together with the confining restriction of visability, emphasized the remoteness of their location.

Mitchell rolled over inside his sleeping bag and stretched luxuriously, emitting several appropriate guttural utterances. He unzipped the sleeping bag and stood up. The cold morning air surprised him. He snatched his clothing from the foot of the sleeping bag. He dressed quickly, the vapor from his breath showing in the morning air. Several yards away Walker lay, still sleeping. Mitchell rolled up his bag and secured it below his pack. He leaned the pack against a tree and walked to the edge of the ridge and sat on a slab of rock above the slope that dropped off into the valley below. The rock was slightly moist from the fog but Mitchell sat anyway and stared out into the haze.

Eventually, the mist began to clear as the sun rose higher and burned it off the mountainside. Below Mitchell, to the east, an immense valley extended for several miles. Beyond it, huge snow-capped peaks stood as sentinels guarding the privacy of the valley. Mitchell saw that he and Walker had camped on a ridge that wound its way along the side of another chain of tall peaks. He could see the snow, not too much higher above them, lodged in the crags and crevices, covering progressively more of the mountain tops as the elevation increased, finally capping them with only small areas of jutting rock left uncovered.

The sun was becoming warmer now. The songs of birds could occasionally be heard ascending from the valley. Behind him, Walker stirred.

"Good morning," Mitchell said.

"Good morning, Eric."

"Fog's lifting . . . looks like it'll be a nice day."

Walker glanced at his watch. "Been up long?"

"About an hour. Anything to eat in your pack?"

"Nothing with me." Walker quickly dressed, and secured his pack. He pointed along the ridge. "Camp's only a few miles from here. We'll walk in and then have breakfast."

Mitchell attached his pack and Walker was studying his compass and a contour map he took from inside his jacket. "Looks like we can follow this ridge for a couple of miles. . . then cross over here. . . ." He indicated a comparative low point in a saddle between two peaks. "From there we'll be less than a mile away." He continued to examine the map. "Does that seem like the best way to you, Mitchell?"

Mitchell flashed a glance at Walker and didn't respond.

Walker smiled, pleased that he hadn't taken the trap. "Let's move out, Eric," he said.

They made good time moving along the ridge in daylight and by eight-thirty had crossed over the ridge they had been paralleling, and began to maneuver their way slowly down the other side into a heavily forested valley. It was not an immense valley such as the one on the opposite side of the ridge, but was rather one that was enclosed on all sides by towering granite spires that haphazardly encircled the two square mile area and then rejoined the predominent chain that twisted its way southward. Beyond the far rim of the valley Mitchell could see another prevalent line in the mountains, with snow-capped crowns paralleling those which they were traversing, and beyond that, yet another. As they descended into the valley, the distant ranges gradually became obscurred by the wall that formed the nearby western boundary, until finally, everything beyond the valley was blotted from view.

It was a rugged area, thick with trees and strewn with rocks and fallen timber and it was a tough route to the bottom. They worked past a sheer rock wall that began as a gradual incline and then dropped off precipitously some hundred feet to the valley floor. At a relatively short distance beyond the drop, the contour of the land sloped off, allowing them adequate footing to make their way to the bottom.

It was an almost eerie feeling in the valley. The dense pines, interspersed with occasional clumps of aspen, towered above them, nearly obliterating any outside view. In spots where the foliage allowed a visual opening, the wall of mountains loomed in stoic silence. The sunlight had not yet penetrated the valley floor, and as Mitchell looked at the intersecting branches high above him, he decided it probably never did to any great degree. There would be only relatively short periods of time each day when the surrounding mountains wouldn't block off the sun. Consequently, it was considerably darker now than it had been on the ridge above. Mitchell could hear the sounds of a stream nearby and a murmur of wind in the pines above, but nothing else. They stopped for a moment upon reaching the bottom.

"I don't particularly look forward to climbing back out of here."

Walker laughed. "Don't worry. When you leave here you'll be able to run to the top with me on your back." He pointed to their right through the trees. "Just a little further."

They moved on deeper into the pines. There was a moist pleasant smell from the earth below and pine needles cushioned their feet. Momentarily they reached the stream which Mitchell had heard, a pebble-lined, crystal-clear creek, flowing quickly toward the southwest. Walker jumped the stream and Mitchell followed. They walked along the bank for another quarter-mile. Then, to the left, tucked behind the base of a grass covered knoll some twenty yards from the creek, and nearly hidden in the surrounding trees, Walker pointed out what Mitchell imagined must have been an old abandoned miner's cabin. The wood was weathered and beaten and the shingles on the roof were in obvious disrepair.

"This is it," Walker gestured. "Our home for the next few weeks."

Mitchell looked it over for a moment and shrugged. "Guess I've stayed in worse," he muttered.

Two wooden steps led onto a sagging porch that fronted the width of the cabin. Walker stopped at the door, took a key from his front pocket and unlocked the door.

74

"We've done a little work on the interior," he said.

Indeed they had. No effort toward elegance had been made, but then this was hardly the place for it. The contrast between inside and out was complete. From the outside, a deserted and dilapidated cabin . . . from the inside, a comfortable mountain cottage, recently and comfortably furnished. The inside walls on all sides were walnut paneled. Newly laid blue tile covered the floor. A fireplace occupied the center of the west wall. A couch, two chairs and an end table bordered a gold throw rug in front of the fireplace. On the other side of the room stood a stove, sink and kitchen table. Wooden cupboards were fastened to the wall above the stove. There were two doors in the wall opposite the front entrance, leading from the main room. One opened to the bathroom, which Mitchell gratefully noted was complete with shower, and the other to a rather plain bedroom containing two army cots, a large clothes rack centered against the wall between the two beds, and two unfinished dressers that stood on either side of the door. There was one curtained window in the bedroom.

They unhooked their packs and let them slide to the floor.

Walker excused himself for a moment and Mitchell stretched out on the cot nearest the door. He closed his eyes and breathed deeply in satisfaction that they were finally here. He was about to wonder where Walker had gone when the sound of a reluctant, sputtering gasoline engine from behind the cabin answered his question. It coughed and gasped for several minutes. He heard Walker swearing at it. Then suddenly it took hold, unwillingly at first, then finally yielding into a smooth rhythmical drone. Walker came back into the cabin.

"Well, what do you think, Werner?"

"All the comforts of home. . . ."

"Take a look at this." Walker moved back into the

main room and Mitchell got off the cot and followed. A large area rug similar to the one in front of the fireplace covered the center of the room. Walker grasped the edge and folded it halfway back. Underneath, the floor appeared the same as it did elsewhere, and the thin line between tiles was indiscernible until Walker gently pried up a corner of one tile and lifted it out of place. He did the same to the tiles flanking it on both sides and then removed the two adjacent rows of three, revealing an area of approximately three square feet.

A heavy metal plate with key holes at both ends comprised the exposed portion of floor. The plate was sunken so that its surface equaled the level of the remainder of the floor when the tiles were replaced. Walker, using two separate keys, released the locks at both ends of the plate. He lifted a recessed handle from one end and motioned Mitchell to do likewise on the other.

It was remarkably heavy and it was with some effort that they lifted the steel door and set it to the side.

"Gently," cautioned Walker. He pointed out the tips of ten separate steel prongs, each a half inch in diameter, spaced at intervals along the sides of the door.

"If this door takes a blow, or is jimmied in some way, these prongs shoot out four inches into the holes you see here. . . ." He indicated ten evenly spaced holes in the steel frame in the floor from which the door had been removed. "And if that happened, it would take a hell of a lot more than we have here to get this thing off."

Mitchell agreed. The heavy steel frame that housed the trap door was several inches thick, and the cross section of floor that was revealed now showed it encased in concrete at least a foot in depth.

Walker lowered himself into the hole and flipped a light switch.

"Come on down, Eric."

Mitchell dropped to the lower level. It was a small room, all concrete and without color. The area was only ten feet square and six feet deep. Walker ducked as he crossed to the far wall.

There were two items in the room. The first, secured by a standard military padlock, was a large metal case approximately three times the size of a foot locker.

"Training supplies," said Walker.

The other object was a safe. The dial and the face were actually quite small, but they were engulfed in a massive slab of concrete that nearly reached the ceiling above and that measured in width and breadth every bit as great as in height.

"If you thought that door up there might be hard to break into, just let me say this puts it to shame. It's time locked, key locked, combination locked."

"What's in there?"

"Exact details of the mission . . . we'll be getting to them as we progress in other areas."

Walker opened the metal case and pulled out a rifle. He tossed it toward Mitchell who caught it with a resounding slap of his palm against the stock. Mitchell handled it crisply, expertly, turning and examining it, pulling the bolt back and letting it slam home with the deft ease and familiarity with which a sculptor might handle his tools.

"The little black gun," he said.

Walker nodded. "The most effective small arms weapon ever designed for close combat."

"It's been a while since I've seen one of these."

"I realize that. Still, you're hardly a stranger to it. In case you don't know it, your Officer Candidate School qualifying score from nearly eight years back still stands as an Army record for the M-16."

Mitchell remembered the day he had scored it with

satisfaction. It had been one of the few times the company tactical officers had shown any emotion. He received letters of commendation and congratulations from the Battalion Commander and the Commanding General of the post.

Walker tapped the end of the barrel. "As you can see, we've equipped it with a silencer . . . often makes things easier for someone in our line of work . . . not to mention keeping our training noise to a minimum. A shot in this valley would echo for an hour."

Mitchell ejected the empty magazine, turned it in his hand, testing the spring with his thumb, then fit it back in place and thrust it into locked position.

"We have a scope for it too. I'll attach it a little later." Walker was sorting through the chest and removing several items. "Have you fired any weapons since the war?"

"No."

"Well, I don't think it'll take you long to reacquaint yourself with it."

Walker had produced several silhouette targets, the scope, a tin of ammunition, several books and a wrist watch from the chest. He handed the watch to Mitchell. "This is one of the most accurate watches in the world . . . runs on a small computer . . . guaranteed not to lose or gain more than ten seconds a year. Never take it off."

Walker locked the chest and motioned to Mitchell. "Let's go up."

They put the door back in place and locked it, carefully replaced the tiles and laid the rug back over it. It was just after ten o'clock.

"The biggest drawback to this whole damn business, Eric, is that we have to do our own cooking." He took out bacon and eggs and set them on the counter. "But I'm hungry enough now that it won't make much difference who cooks it. We'll switch off . . . I'll cook today, you take tomorrow."

THE MAN ON THE LEFT

* * *

After breakfast they went out with the silhouettes several hundred yards from the cabin near the eastern wall of the valley. The trees were more sparse in that area and after a short search, Walker located an area that provided a staggered opening through the trees for a distance of slightly over a hundred yards. At given points along the line there was as much as twenty yards spacing between trees, in others as little as five feet. At the base of the mountain on the east end of the valley they firmly staked down the targets, then walked off a hundred yards back through the firing lane and staked that point. Looking back through the trees the targets stood motionless, blending with the greenery surrounding them.

"Good," said Walker. "Now we're going to set up something that you won't enjoy quite as much as this."

"Which is. . . ."

"An obstacle course. You'll run it twice a day."

Natural surroundings provided the obstacles—fallen trees, the creek, several small knolls at the base of the valley's south wall. Walker was thorough and precise in laying out the most difficult route he could find. At intervals he drove white tipped stakes into the ground to mark the way.

"I make it about two miles," he judged as the cabin once again came into view.

They finished settling and arranging things in the cabin and later in the afternoon they went to the firing range.

"We won't spend a lot of time here today . . . just zero in your weapon and that will take care of it."

Mitchell took up a prone position at the one-hundred yard stake. He snugged the stock against his cheek and sighted downrange through the scope. It felt as natural and familiar in his grasp as an old girl friend. He nudged the selector on semi-automatic, locked the magazine in place and chambered the first round.

Walker was speaking as Mitchell applied a steadily increasing pressure on the trigger.

"Fire a pattern of ten and we'll check it."

With a muffled "chuk," the M-16 recoiled and the first round ripped into the upper left hand corner of the body of the silhouette.

"It's left a little," Mitchell said, still sighting down the scope. "Elevation's about right."

"How does it feel to you?"

"Like part of my arm."

He fired another round that nearly passed through the same hole as the first. Without the benefit of the scope, Walker couldn't see where the target was being hit.

"Same place?"

"Uh-huh." Mitchell fired again. "Just needs a turn or two right windage. Elevation is perfect."

"Well, go ahead and shoot the full ten. We'll go up then and take a look to be sure."

Mitchell squeezed off the next seven shots in quick succession, allowing only a momentary pause for recoil before sending the next round on its way.

"I want you to take your time on this," Walker admonished him as they started down range to inspect the target. "You'll have plenty of opportunity to fire for speed. It's important right now to get a right pattern to zero the weapon in."

"Have you got a half-dollar?"

Walker laughed. "Sorry, I don't. Do you think that would cover it?"

"Maybe all we'll need is a quarter."

"I think I only have a dime."

"Save it for the next pattern."

Walker stuck his finger through the hole in the target and emitted a low whistle. Not a single round had landed outside the tight grouping.

"That's fantastic," said Walker. "You haven't fired a weapon in years and you group a pattern like that." He motioned at the silhouette and shook his head. "And you squeezed off those last seven almost as fast as you could pull the trigger."

Mitchell was pleased with himself, and with Walker's obvious respect for his skill.

Mitchell took a quarter from his pocket and held it up to the target. Only a portion of the hole made by one round extended over the top right-hand edge of the coin.

"Must have been the one you were talking on."

They both laughed loudly and turned and walked back to the marker.

Mitchell made a slight windage adjustment on the scope and fired ten more rounds, all bunched into the middle of the head of the silhouette.

"Take a look," he said to Walker.

Walker sighted through the scope. So perfect was the pattern that from their vantage point it appeared as if only one high caliber hole had been put in the silhouette. Walker thought to himself that this man must certainly be one of the greatest marksmen in the world.

"What will you do after a little practice?" he laughed. Walker handed the weapon back to Mitchell. "I don't really see any point in our going down for a closer look."

They pocketed the brass cartridge casings and moved back toward the cottage. Walker was silently marveling what he regarded as the greatest exhibition of small arms firing he'd ever seen. "You know," he mused, as they moved up the stairs and inside the cabin, "I really believe a dime would have covered that last pattern."

At 1600 Hours that day, Mitchell underwent his first session of physical training. Walker, leading the exercises, proved every bit as fit as he appeared. After thirty minutes of grueling, non-stop calisthenics that left Mitchell gasping for breath, they moved directly to the obstacle course where Walker ran abreast of Mitchell for half the distance, urging, chiding, compelling, insulting him to pick up the pace. Mitchell's chest heaved in the thin air and his breath came in hot, stabbing gasps. He wanted to quit but pride wouldn't allow him to be run into the ground by a man twenty years his senior.

"Can't you set any faster pace than this?" he yelled hoarsely after another of Walker's taunts.

"Just watch me!" Walker shouted over his shoulder.

Mitchell cursed him as he disappeared into the trees ahead. He continued running now only as a reflex action ... legs pumping mechanically ... aching. When he finally stumbled across the end line, Walker, who had been resting against the trunk of a nearby tree stood and checked his watch.

"Eighteen minutes." He shook his head. "Leaves a little room for improvement."

Mitchell's head was reeling and his chest was afire. The high altitude exertion seemed twice as strenuous as it might have at a lower elevation, and in conjunction with Mitchell's relative inactivity over the past several years, he felt the combination might well do him in. He couldn't control the loud rasping that accompanied his gulped breaths.

"Mountain air really perks you up, doesn't it?" Walker gestured. "Makes me feel like going around again."

Mitchell hurt too much to answer.

"You going to be all right?"

Mitchell shook his head.

"I'll go in and get some food cooking. Walk it off."

Mitchell made no response. Walker unlocked the cabin and went inside. Mitchell walked a short distance into the trees, sank to his hands and knees and vomited. Even after the contents of his stomach was emptied, the process continued until his guts ached throughout. His head pounded from the lack of oxygen.

When he finally brought his stomach under control he rose and walked it off, breathing deeply of the air that had begun cooling rapidly now as the sun disappeared behind the valley wall.

It was almost an hour before he went inside the cabin. They had a good meal but Mitchell could only pick at it. By eight o'clock that night, he was asleep.

Morning came too quickly for Mitchell, and by seven-thirty they were once again in the midst of the same exhausting exercise routine. Mitchell had the good sense to attempt to pace himself this time. Even so, Walker pushed him to the extent that it took an effort to fight off the nausea that welled up within him after completion of the obstacle course.

It was Mitchell's turn to cook. While he scrambled eggs and cooked bacon, Walker sat at the table and set down an approximate training schedule.

"We'll make changes in this if it suits us," Walker said. "But for openers, we'll adhere to this."

Mitchell took the sheet of paper that Walker handed him and studied it.

    0700—Wake up
    0730-0830—Physical training
    0900-0930—Breakfast
    0930-1130—Weapons firing
    1130-1200—Hand to hand combat
    1200-1300—Lunch
    1300-1600—Review of German culture, lifestyle,
                    etc.
    1600-1700—Physical training
    1800—Dinner

He handed it back with no comment.

"We want you ready in several ways, Eric," Walker said. "We want you in top physical condition; we want you to be as good as you possibly can with your weapon and in self defense techniques; and we want you updated on the Germany of today. There have been changes— small perhaps, but important nonetheless—little things that would single you out as not being a German national."

"How long do we do this?"

"Until I'm satisfied that you're ready in each one of the ways I mentioned. We won't rush it. If you're lacking in any one area, it could cost your life . . . or you might blow the mission."

Mitchell looked up from scraping the eggs from the skillet onto two plates.

"The point I'm making is to take all this seriously. It sounds trite but it's a matter of life and death to you."

"Haven't I been serious enough?"

Walker took the plate of bacon, eggs, and toast and poured a large glass of milk. "You've done well. Don't let up. I know getting in shape isn't an easy thing to do, but push yourself. You'll be the better for it."

"You don't have to sell me, Walker. If I didn't believe it was important I'd be an ass to be here at all." Mitchell pulled up his chair and began working on the plate before him. "I'll give you a hundred percent, Walker. Don't worry about it."

Walker smiled to himself. "All right, I won't," he said.

The morning's session at the firing range proved that the previous day's success was no fluke. By the session's end, one of the silhouettes had been obliterated. In reality, had they wanted to, they could have used one silhouette for several weeks. So expert was Mitchell with the M-16, he could put every round inside a previously fired pattern.

But it was no fun to put a round through another hole, so Walker had taken a piece of chalk and marked one inch circles in rows and files across the first silhouette. Mitchell had methodically begun with the top left circle and eliminated each one in turn, in the process rendering the silhouette a shambles of uniform perforations.

The morning hand-to-hand combat session was divided into two parts. The first, a review by Walker of pressure points, vital spots, kicks, gouges, stomps, take-downs, counter measures to use against the aforementioned, and other assorted acts of mayhem. The second stage was an intense practical application of the principles involved in both hand-to-hand attack and defense. Mitchell had never been particularly proficient in the art of hand-to-hand combat and it grated on him when Walker threw him so effortlessly while he had to strain and curse and probably get a little cooperation to get Walker off his feet.

The afternoon schedule consisted of the most comprehensive crash course in German culture, tradition, history, language, governmental structure, social characteristics, and philosophy that could be condensed into a three hour period.

Walker held up a copy of the *U.S. Army—Area Handbook for Germany*. "This will be our text and the basis for our discussions on the German way of life. I've spent a lot of time in researching this and I've picked out about six hours of the most pertinent information." He handed the book to Mitchell. "We'll cover three hours today—the second half tomorrow."

"Only two days to spend on that?"

"The third day, we start over again. We'll cover and recover all essential material until we'll nearly be able to recite it."

And so it went. Occasionally after dinner, Walker spent some time talking on a telephone that had been among the equipment in the underground vault. Mitchell didn't know to whom the calls were directed, but after the second call, Walker informed him that his car had been pulled from the Blue Mountain Reservoir and he had been listed as missing and presumed dead.

The calls were made from the vault area, and even though Mitchell tuned an attentive ear in that direction, he managed to hear only snatches of conversation. In one instance he thought he heard Walker ask how "Younger" was doing. He considered questioning Walker about it, but decided against it.

The days passed routinely. It had been exciting at first, but the repetition of activity day after day soon began to lose its novelty. It took a greater effort for Mitchell to apply himself and still Walker had given him no further specifics relative to the mission.

Some good had come of it, however. Mitchell noted with a sense of satisfaction that his body was responding to the physical training. The hint of excess weight that had begun gathering at his waist over the past several years had turned solid now, and the brisk runs through the valley obstacle course were exhilarating rather than exhausting. After the end of the first week, Walker had stopped running the obstacle course with Mitchell. Mitchell believed it was because Walker knew it was only a matter of time before Mitchell would be able to overtake and beat him through the course.

He had fired thousands of rounds with the M-16— standing, squatting, prone, sitting, kneeling. There was virtually no way he could improve upon his marksmanship and Walker was aware of it.

As Walker had promised, they'd nearly committed the Army handbook on Germany to memory. They had spoken the German language exclusively for such a long time that Mitchell sometimes found his thoughts being formed in German. They had spent a great amount of time in the evenings updating his use of the language, spicing it with modern phrases and old colloquialisms. As a result he had a more authentic command of the language than ever before.

Only twice was the training routine altered, that being in the past two days. They had taken an hour from target practice and a half hour from hand-to-hand combat, and made their way to the sheer cliffs near where they had originally descended into the valley. They spent the time rappelling down the perpendicular stone surfaces. "It's good exercise," Walker said. "And you never know when it may come in handy."

Mitchell eventually lost track of time. One evening after he estimated they'd been there for two weeks, he put it directly to Walker.

"How much longer?"

Walker was sitting on the couch leafing through a magazine. He closed it and threw it on the end table.

"Do you think you're ready yet?"

"Yes."

"No doubts?"

"I'm ready! What do I do? And when do I do it?"

Walker studied Mitchell for only a few seconds. "We'll leave here in three days."

The nearly instantaneous reply took Mitchell a bit by surprise. "When did you decide this?"

"Just now," Walker said. "Oh, I had an idea when we

came here, but we had to be a little flexible . . . had to make sure you'd be ready. And of course, the timing had to be right in Germany—we'll leave in three days."

Mitchell wondered what Walker meant about the timing in Germany, but he felt a sense of relief at knowing something more definite about when things were going to happen.

"And I guess it's about time we covered a few specifics," Walker said. He folded back the area rug in the center of the floor. "Give me a hand with this, will you?"

Together, they pulled the heavy cover aside and Walker dropped into the vault below.

Chapter 10.

The file that lay on the table was covered by a type-written classification jacket that read:

TOP SECRET-SPECIAL CLASSIFICATION

Contains information vital to the defense of the United States. Disclosure of this information would seriously jeopardize national security.

To be read by the following three individuals only:

The President of the United States

Walker, Franklin N.

Mitchell, David R.

Because of the extremely sensitive nature of the material contained herein, this document has been specially classified and will not be covered by normal file and classification procedures. Document is to be destroyed after above authorized individuals have seen it. No other copy exists.

TOP SECRET-SPECIAL CLASSIFICATION

Mitchell re-read it several times. He had never seen anything classified in such a manner.

Walker rolled the rug back over the trap door and smoothed it with his foot. He took a seat across the kitchen table from Mitchell.

"You'd think they could design a more impressive cover for a classification as important as this." Mitchell was referring to the simple white cardboard cover, upon which the classification information was typed.

"Does look a little homemade, doesn't it? I guess we don't use that particular classification often enough to merit any creative effort. That might be a good project for an ex-ad man."

Walker unclipped the classification cover from the attached manila folder. The typewritten words, "Project Red Ruler" were centered on the folder.

"We'll take it from the top, Eric." Walker settled into the chair, pulled a pack of cigarettes from his shirt pocket and flipped them on the table. "We had a man in Germany for over five years. He was relatively quiet for those five years . . . nothing of any importance had ever come up. Even so, we felt it was important to have someone in that area. And eventually," gestured Walker, "he did stumble on to something . . . by accident really . . . something he didn't pay much attention to at first."

Mitchell leaned forward with his elbows on the table and listened.

"It looked like just another lunatic fringe group. Like a half dozen others, it appealed to the individual German's nationalist loyalty, and to his desire for the unification of the two Germanys. Our man knew about this organization for well over a year before he ever took it seriously."

"What happened to change his mind?" Mitchell asked.

"As I said, it took some time. He was stationed in Munich for over two years . . . had a cover established as an antique dealer in the *Viktualienmarkt*. He'd heard mention of the group, and after dropping his name to a few of the right people, became a member. It was a far-out group, passive at the time he first discovered it, but with some pretty ambitious plans." Walker took a cigarette from the pack on the table. "But our man didn't take them seriously enough back then to do any more than just report the existence of the group."

"Why not?"

"Numbers. They were such a small unit that he felt they couldn't do much more than provide themselves with diversions from their everyday routines . . . even though the people involved seemed to have a greater sense of purpose than you might expect from such a group."

"What finally made him decide to take them seriously?"

"We had to send him to Hamburg on a mission . . . nothing special, just something routine we wanted to check out. One night in a beer garden, he overheard two men talking. One of them mentioned this group. He struck up a conversation and eventually, over a period of nearly a year, got inside the group in Hamburg."

Mitchell considered what Walker had said. "Why couldn't he identify himself as a member of the organization in Munich and save the problem of working his way inside?"

"He was using a different name in Hamburg." Walker lit his cigarette and inhaled thoughtfully. "Actually it turned out that his second identity probably saved his life."

Mitchell's expression asked for an explanation.

"When he was a member of the Munich group, he'd never heard mention of any other faction being located anywhere else. And after being a member of the Hamburg group for a short time, it became evident that they weren't aware of the branch in Munich."

Mitchell nodded. "That *would* make you stop and think."

"Our man spent the next several months trying to establish some ties from one group to the other. He found the organization of both groups was similar . . . relatively small units of between seventy-five and a hundred people . . . a membership that was very select . . . people from all types of backgrounds, all decidedly above average . . . no run-of-the-mill political dissidents . . . and *all* strong German nationalists who didn't have much good to say about the current West German government."

Walker butted his cigarette in the ashtray and continued talking. "Still, we didn't have any concrete evidence that related the groups to one another. But about six months later, our agent overheard the man in charge of the Hamburg organization refer to a message he'd received. A code name was involved. Our man had heard the same code used in Munich. Eventually, he learned the code referred to the man who set the policies and made the decisions for the group . . . the absolute and final authority on everything that happened . . and that man had control over *both* groups!"

"Yet neither group was aware of the other?"

"Apparently not." Walker paused shortly and then went on. "This left us with several things to work on. Who was this guy? How serious was the threat? Were there any more cells in existence in other cities?"

Walker rose and propped one foot on the edge of his chair. "So we sent him to Frankfurt, Bonn, Cologne, Berlin. We found that every major city in West Germany contained a faction of this group. And not a single unit was aware of the existence of any other!"

Mitchell whistled softly. "And the same man controlled them all?"

"The same man," Walker said.

"So, from what your man originally thought was one small group of malcontents, he found a network of top-notch people covering the entire country."

"Exactly. It was evident now that we were dealing with what could be a very potent force, provided they were all brought together. We had to identify the man and find out what he was up to before something happened."

Mitchell shook his head in disbelief. "It's hard to imagine what an organizer a man would have to be to set up a situation like that."

"He's quite a man, there's no doubt about that," Walker agreed. "After we'd finally identified him, we found that he'd organized each unit through one man in each city. He handpicked these men himself and entrusted them with developing and running their groups according to his dictates."

"And he remained anonymous except to those men in charge of each unit?"

"Right. Members of the group were aware that directions came from another source, but no one knew who it was."

"Wouldn't that make it difficult to get their support?" Mitchell asked.

"No," Walker said. "The men in charge of each unit were truly outstanding people in their own right . . . the top man saw to that . . . and they in turn saw to the quality that they allowed inside their groups."

Mitchell was fascinated. "How long did it take to organize this thing?"

"Probably about ten years. They may still be in the process of adding units today." Walker thought for a moment. "I guess the most amazing thing about it is how this group has kept its secrecy by being selective about who they take in. We'd never even heard a rumor of it until our man happened to get inside." His tone of voice indicated the professional respect he had for his adversaries. He stood reflecting on it for a moment in silence.

"What happened next?" Mitchell asked.

Walker turned back to him. "We sent our man back to Munich. It seemed like the group there was as active as any, and he'd been a member there for some time. He got back into the group under his old cover, and eventually, he discovered the identity of the top man."

Mitchell waited for the name, but Walker didn't offer it.

"Our agent then went on a personal campaign to be the most outstanding individual in the Munich group. No one worked longer or harder or with more determination than he did. And after a matter of time, he became the closest friend and confidant of the man in charge of the cell. Through him, he found out the plans of the head man. He found that the ultimate purpose of the cell was to seize control of the communications and governmental facilities of Munich, when so directed by the head man. The cell leader told our agent that this was something that would take place within the next few years. The group began reviewing in earnest the steps required to achieve their objective. The cell leader knew only that the action would be initiated by the head man, and that it would be in conjunction with another effort elsewhere within the country. He had no idea that cells such as his own existed throughout the country."

"And that was enough for him? Just to know that's what the number one man wanted?"

"That's where the real strength of this organization comes from. Remember, these cell leaders are handpicked. They're dedicated. They don't ask questions." Walker pushed his chair back and sat down again. "By taking a few business trips, our man found that each cell across the country had the same mission in their own city that the Munich group had in Munich."

"So," said Mitchell, "at a given notice, these specialized groups from all over the country would seize control of every major city in West Germany."

"That's right," Walker agreed. "Still, we needed more information. Our agent had identified the number one man, and finally, after several more months, managed to get a bug on his phone and photograph a document or two. What he learned from those things made everything beforehand seem insignificant."

"What was it?"

"Two things really," Walker said. "We found that a cell similar to those in each city existed in the German Army . . . and we learned that the head man communicated regularly with another foreign power. The idea behind the whole thing wasn't only to change the German form of government . . . it was to change the balance of power in Europe."

Mitchell leaned back in his chair and emitted a loud sigh. The potential impact was monumental.

"And changing the balance of power in Europe," Mitchell said, "would change the balance of power in the world."

"And in this case, drastically for the worse," Walker said. "As an ex-military man, I don't have to tell you how politicians have let our armed forces deteriorate since Vietnam. While they've had their heads in the sand, a gradual realignment in the balance of world power has begun. We've sacrificed military preparedness for half-assed attempts to balance a budget that no one really understands or gives a shit about. Countries that were third rate powers ten years ago are developing some pretty sophisticated weapons systems. Our allies have gone soft. We've gone soft. Instead of being lean and hungry, we're fat and sassy. Those countries that still have a commitment . . . a cause . . . won't pussyfoot around when they think their time has come. And if a nation with the industrial power and the technological advancement of Germany gets into bed with another major power . . ." Walker threw up his hands in a gesture of helplessness. "The pure and simple truth now is that we might not be able to do anything about a situation like this once it's occurred." Walker tapped the table to emphasize his point. "That's why our job—seeing to it that it doesn't happen again—is all important. It's hard to foresee everything that might happen, but our best projections, based on what we know about this man and the country he's allied with, indicates war of some sort would be inevitable." Walker shrugged his shoulders. "It could start off right with the attempted takeover. If things went badly there, the top man's ally might step in to help—that could bring a response from other countries. Before you know it, it would be out of control. On the other hand, if the coup were successful, we're looking at a direct threat that could only get stronger."

"What's the general philosophy of this group?" asked Mitchell.

"Communist," Walker said. "Actually it's a conglomeration of sorts. Remnants of several different groups . . . German Reich Party, Socialist Reich Party, Federal Deutsche Party . . . but the top level is Communist."

Mitchell was still marveling at the entire situation. "How could they pull together divergent groups like that into one cooperative force?"

"I guess the main reason is a common sense of purpose. The leading people from these various organizations have long since recognized the fact that they lacked the strength to achieve their goals. For the people who have spent a lifetime working towards those goals, this new group offered an opportunity.

"Of course, the driving force behind this outfit is the top man." Walker got up and retrieved the Army Handbook on Germany and opened it to a section concerned with subversive groups. "When this book was written, the Army evaluated the likelihood of any type of coalition as pretty remote. The only possibility they could foresee that might lead to a coalition was a crises of some type. Even under those circumstances they said any coalition was unlikely unless. . ." At this point Walker laid the handbook before Mitchell and pointed out the line as he read it. ". . . unless one strong leader could pull them together."

"And that's what's happened," said Mitchell.

"Over the last several months, cases of civil disturbances have increased tremendously throughout the country. While we can't trace it specifically, we feel it's this group, stepping up their activities to create the general unrest that will eventually end with their move to take over."

Mitchell had scarcely moved throughout the entire, unbelievable explanation. He stood now and walked to the window where he peered into the darkness. "If all this took place—even considering the extent of the organization—would the German people stand for it?"

"To answer that, you have to consider several points," Walker said. "First, *all* Germans believe Germany should be united. The fact that there have been two Germany's for so many years has been a source of discontent there for a long time. Many don't feel the current government has made strong enough efforts in that area. Second, a strong nationalistic feeling and a loyalty to the Fatherland is an inherent German trait, and is one of the things that this group would exploit. And finally, Germans have had a traditional inclination to favor a strong executive form of government. They have a positive attitude towards authority."

"In other words, they might go along with it."

"They might," Walker affirmed. "And even if they don't, the group would have so firm a grip on the country that it probably wouldn't make much difference anyway."

Mitchell stood at the window and reviewed the details in his mind. Walker waited a moment and then continued again.

"So, Eric, it became imperative that we take some action." Walker slid his chair closer to the table and opened the file. "Which brings us to you."

Mitchell remained at the window a moment, then turned slowly and sat once again at the table. "Is the agent that discovered this outfit still a member of it?"

"No."

"Why not?"

"He's dead," Walker said.

The news gave Mitchell a start. "What happened?"

"After we'd learned what we wanted about the group, we thought it would be a good idea to get the bug off the phone before the top man accidentally found it. We stood to be in a stronger position if he didn't know that anyone was on to his plan."

"Makes sense."

"Our man had just removed the bug early one morning last winter, when he was surprised by a security guard. He was shot trying to escape. They found the bug on him. We hope they assumed he was there to plant it, not remove it. Under the circumstances, it was probably better for our man and for us that he died. They had no way to question him and could only guess whether or not he really knew anything. We think they finally decided he had suspected something, but hadn't gotten the opportunity to learn anything."

"And now you want me to get inside this group."

"Let's get to that right now," Walker said. He turned the first page of the folder, which was a repetition of the classification instructions on the cover. "The mission is known as 'Project Red Ruler'."

Walker flipped through seven or eight typed pages. "I'll skip over this background information that we've just finished talking about and get to the conclusion. From what we've discussed already, it may be rather obvious. Our code name for their number one man is 'Big Red'." Walker flipped the next page. "Your code name is 'Red Eraser'."

The implication was obvious.

"Your mission is to kill him," said Walker flatly.

As Mitchell considered it, he didn't know why it should have surprised him. If he had reviewed the training—firing with a scope and silencer, the nature of the enemy organization—he might have guessed as much. Certainly the thought must have crossed his mind. Still when it was laid out so starkly before him, it required an effort at nonchalance. Walker could sense it.

"Of course something like this isn't easy. It's one thing to shoot a man in combat—quite another to shoot one on the street." Walker tapped the table for emphasis. "The thing we have to keep in proper perspective is that this man is the greatest threat to world peace since World War II. To put it another way, the fate of the world might depend on this man's death. Without it, everything might go up for grabs. With him out of the way, the organization is no longer a threat. He's the only thing that binds it together and gives it power. Without him, it becomes only small, unrelated groups of dissidents with no means of achieving their purpose. With his influence gone, we feel the group members will eventually become disenchanted, and the cells will break up."

Mitchell was making a concerted effort to pull his thoughts together. For over an hour his mind had been bombarded with information that must have been the most critical in the free world. And when it seemed finally about to fall in place, this final explosive point had been driven home, momentarily shattering his detached appraisal of the situation.

It was several minutes before he spoke. When he did, it was with the conviction of one who has weighed the evidence and arrived at a decision.

"All right," he said. "How do I go about it?"

Walker's face mirrored relief at Mitchell's decision. "There's one other man involved in this," he said.

Mitchell looked up in surprise. "Another man?"

"You'll never see him. He'll keep in touch with you. It's his job to set the thing up. He'll tell you when, where, and how it's to be done."

Mitchell didn't quite buy it. "You mean I'm the man who will actually do it, but I don't have anything to say about the setup?"

"That's right."

"I don't like it!"

"Listen, Eric," Walker said, "you're an expert in your phase of it—you're perfectly qualified to do the job. We couldn't find anyone else who'd fit in better." Walker shifted his weight in the chair. "The same thing goes for the set-up man. He's a pro. Nobody could do it as well. Not me . . . and not you."

Mitchell reluctantly agreed. "I suppose so. I just don't like the idea of someone else having that much control over it."

"Give me a little credit, too," Walker said. "If there was a better way to set this thing up, I'd have thought of it."

"I suppose you would have."

"Hey," Walker said, changing his tone to a lighter vein, "why don't we pop a couple of beers from the refrigerator?"

"Are you kidding?" They hadn't had anything to drink since arriving in the valley, and to Mitchell's knowledge, there wasn't anything alcoholic on hand.

"I've been saving it. Seems like this might be a good time."

Mitchell opened the refrigerator. Two cases of cold Coors jammed the bottom two shelves. "I'll be damned," he said. He grabbed two cans and set them on the table. "Where the hell have you been hiding this?"

Walker opened his beer and took a long draw. "In the safe." They both laughed, and finished off a beer quickly and Mitchell got another. They drank silently for several minutes.

"Who is my contact?" Mitchell asked.

"There's really no need for you to know, but in case something comes up later and for some reason you *have* to know . . . your contact's name is Gus. I won't tell you any more than that."

"How will we do it?"

"That much is fairly certain . . . barring some unforeseen occurrence, you'll use the same M-16 you've trained on."

"How do we get it over there?"

"Not your problem. It'll be there when you need it."

"What about zeroing it?" Mitchell said. "You can't take a weapon across the ocean without getting it out of adjustment."

"Believe me, when you pick it up in Germany, it'll be

exactly like it was the last time you fired it. That's a guarantee!"

Mitchell took another swallow. "So I'll leave in three days, huh?"

"We'll pack out of here day after tomorrow. You'll fly to New York City and then to Stuttgart. From there, you'll take a train to Munich." Walker crushed a can in his large hand. "Then you'll wait."

"I guess there's only one more question," said Mitchell, looking intently at Walker.

"And what would that be?"

"Who is Big Red?" asked Mitchell.

"Doesn't make any difference, Eric. You wouldn't know him anyway."

"You're asking a hell of a lot," protested Mitchell. "You're asking me to kill a man and you won't even tell me who it is."

"That's right," Walker said, "we are asking a hell of a lot! That's part of the deal. But you don't need to know the man's name. You know what he is; that's all that counts."

Mitchell wasn't satisfied, but it was obvious that Walker had nothing further to say on the matter.

"How about another beer?" Walker said. He retrieved them and set one before Mitchell. Walker then reached inside the file and produced a business envelope. "There are a few things here that should interest you." He handed the envelope to Mitchell.

There were three things inside. One was a telephone number.

"Memorize it," said Walker. "Then burn it. And remember one thing about it . . . never call that number unless you're instructed to."

Mitchell studied the number. "Got it," he said. He crumpled the paper, walked across the room and dropped it in the fireplace.

The second item was a Swiss bank receipt. Mitchell whistled quietly under his breath as he counted the zeroes that followed the number "one". One hundred thousand dollars!"

"That should make things a little easier when you get back," Walker said. "Of course we'll keep you in spending money while you're in Germany."

The third item was a letter. It was both forthright and concise.

Dear Mr. Mitchell:

You have just made the biggest decision of your life. Several weeks ago, I too, was called upon to make that decision. I applaud you for having accepted this difficult task.

Few man are called to serve in such a critical situation. While some seemingly distasteful actions are difficult to perform, we must recognize the good of our great nation, as well as that of all mankind, and act accordingly.

I salute you for your dedication and courage. Your actions will serve the cause of worldwide peace.

It was signed by the President of the United States.

Mitchell read the letter several times. Finally, he rose and walked again to the fireplace. "It's suitable for framing, but then I guess that wouldn't be using good judgment." He watched the flames consume the letter.

Chapter 11.

On the same day that Mitchell learned the full details of his mission, a man in Berlin named Joseph Springer was preparing for an important meeting.

It was an unscheduled meeting of the Deutscheland Club, a group of seventy-five men that had met on a monthly basis for over five years. Recently they had begun meeting at least twice a month. Their last meeting had been held only four days ago.

There was never an attendance problem with the Deutscheland Club. Its members were devout and tireless workers. This unscheduled meeting, while perhaps inconvenient to many, would not be met with objections and complaints about a lack of advance notice. Like every other meeting, only those who were out of town or ill would miss it.

The credit for this dedication belonged to Joseph Springer. He had personally spent days—sometimes weeks—in a rigorous screening of every member who had joined the club. Most were friends . . . a few were acquaintances or business associates. If he had no personal knowledge of a proposed applicant, it took a strong endorsement from at least four current members before Springer would entertain thoughts of acceptance.

That was the way the original founder of the club had

wanted it. Springer followed his guidelines without wavering.

Joseph Springer was one of Berlin's most prominent attorneys. He was a powerful man with friends in important places. He was the kind of man with the energy and intelligence to get things done.

The meeting that would be held later in the day had been precipitated by another meeting that had taken place the previous evening in Springer's home. Springer had not called that meeting. It was not his place to do so.

It had been past midnight when a car pulled up in Springer's drive. Three people got out.

Springer greeted the familiar figure with open arms. "My friend," he said, embracing him.

"Hello, Joseph," the other man replied. "You look well."

"Come in, come in," said Springer. "Let me take your coat."

They walked into the foyer of Springer's home. The two men accompanying Springer's guest stepped inside with them.

"Do you mind," said Springer's guest, "if my associates look around a bit?" His tone was apologetic. "It embarrasses me to have them do it, but these young fellows are insistent upon following certain procedures. . . ." He shrugged helplessly.

"By all means," said Springer. "I wouldn't have it any other way." He motioned about the house. "Gentlemen, please look around as you see fit."

Without a word the two moved off in opposite directions. Springer and his guest made idle chatter while they waited. In a few moments, both young men had returned. "Sorry for the inconvenience," one of them said to Springer, in a voice that didn't really sound sorry at all.

"Where can we talk, Joseph?" the other man said.

"The study is right off the hallway," Springer said.

"Ah, yes . . . I remember it as a very comfortable and charming room."

"You flatter me," said Springer. "Come . . . it's this way."

One of the young men went outside and stationed himself by the door. The other pulled up a chair in the hallway outside the study.

The two men settled comfortably into two soft brown leather chairs that faced each other. Springer poured two brandies. They sipped their drinks casually for a few moments and reminisced about trivial matters. Springer let his friend lead the conversation. The transition from the education of their children to the matter at hand was smooth.

"These are challenging times for everyone, Joseph," his guest said. "We have some grave responsibilities . . . to our families . . . and to our country." His right eye twitched involuntarily as he spoke . . . a nervous tic that had been with him for nearly all his life.

"I'm committed to those responsibilities," Springer said.

The other nodded his head. "I know you are. That's why you were chosen for the important mission of organizing the group you call the 'Deutscheland Club.' It's an assignment that few men could have accomplished. The quality of your group, their dedication, their sense of purpose . . . all a reflection of your efforts and your ability."

"Thank you," Springer said. "I've been pleased with them. They've never disappointed me."

"We'll be asking a lot from them very shortly, the other replied.

"They're ready to do what I ask," said Springer. He held the brandy bottle up in an offer to refill the glasses, but his guest waved it away. Springer set the bottle aside.

"We're approaching a very important point in history," Springer's guest said. "A critical time not only for Germany, but for the world. We will play key roles. Your group will be vital to the success of our movement." He paused for emphasis. "It's coming faster than we had anticipated. The time is nearly at hand."

Emotions surged within Springer's soul. Tears welled in his eyes. "The time is nearly at hand," he repeated. He said it again as if to convince himself. "It has been many years . . . a lifetime for some of us."

The other nodded. "This is the time for positive action. There can be no turning back now. When your group is called on, you must act. Your function is a part of the overall plan that, like every other part, is essential."

"We're ready," Springer said.

"Call your people together as soon as possible. Intensify your normal training. Review the steps that each man takes in his assignment. Requalify everyone on small arms. Have them cancel any vacation plans for the next two months."

"Will it happen within the next two months?"

"Yes," Springer's guest replied. "Other plans are already in motion. Some startling things will happen in coming weeks . . . things that will grab the attention of the entire world. They're all part of the overall plan."

Springer was too overcome to speak. He had dedicated his life to a cause that was now about to be realized.

His guest stood. "Your unit on civil disobedience should step up their activity during the next two weeks. It's important that the political climate within the country remain unstable."

Springer nodded.

"I wanted to come here in person to tell you that our goal is in sight. Alert your men."

They shook hands and started for the door. "You'll have a twenty-four hour notice, time for you to pull your group together and coordinate your effort."

He opened the door to the study and the young man who had remained in the hallway led them to the front door. Springer's guest walked to his car and got inside. He rolled down the window. "For the Fatherland," he said.

"For the Fatherland." Springer waved as the car rolled down the drive. He stood there for several moments after the car had disappeared. The night was cool. The smell of the air was clean and refreshing. It was very still. He took a deep breath and brushed at his eyes with the back of his hand, then turned to the door. "For the Fatherland," he said quietly.

Chapter 12.

It rained in the Colorado Rockies for the next three days, the first precipitation of the past two weeks. When Mitchell and Walker climbed out of the valley, the footing was slippery and uncertain.

Mitchell moved purposefully over the slick terrain. The moisture served to accent the clean pungency of pine that normally filled the air. Crossing the ridge that bordered the east end of the valley, he felt a refreshing sense of strength that he had not known for too long a time, and the feeling elated him.

Walker checked his map and compass at the top of the ridge. "There's a road beyond that tree line in the distance." He pointed it out as he spoke. "About five miles from here."

Mitchell located the position and nodded. "Just keep moving in line with the roundish peak behind them."

"Right," Walker said. "From there you'll hitch into Denver." Walker was reviewing what they had previously discussed. "Got your plane ticket?"

Mitchell reached inside his pocket and produced the one-way United Airlines ticket to New York.

Walker handed him a key. "After you get to LaGuardia, you open locker number forty-eight, change into a business suit, then go to the Park Lane Hotel, 36 Central Park South."

"The Park Lane," Mitchell repeated. "Everything I need will be waiting there for me."

"I guess you've got it," Walker said. They stood a moment while Walker surveyed him. He stuck out his hand and gave Mitchell a firm handshake. "I think you're ready, Eric."

It was a brief awkward moment when two strong men who had come to respect one another were parting company, and while each would have liked to say something appropriate, it was contrary to both their natures.

"I'll see you," said Mitchell.

"Good luck," said Walker. "Remember . . . do everything exactly as you're instructed. Your contact's a pro . . . just as you are . . . follow his instructions to the letter . . . no questions." Walker slung Mitchell's rifle over his shoulder. "We'll have this there when you need it."

They adjusted their packs.

"Gros glück," said Walker.

"Auf Wiedersehen," said Mitchell.

It was almost noon and the rain had let up when Mitchell slid down a muddy embankment onto the highway and scraped and stomped the mud from his boots. He wondered how long it might take to hitch a ride, but scarcely ten minutes had passed before a sporting goods salesman from Salt Lake City gave him a lift. By six o'clock, Mitchell was airborne, enroute to New York City.

The flight lasted little more than three-and-a-half hours, but the crossing of two time zones made it nearly midnight when the United jet touched down at LaGuardia. Mitchell retrieved his pack from the baggage claim and strode briskly down the corridor to a bank of lockers adjacent to a Hertz rental booth. He put the key into number forty-eight and opened the door. Inside was a shaving kit, one business suit, a shirt and tie, underwear, handkerchief, socks and shoes. A note instructing him to leave his old belongings behind was hung on the hook at the back of the locker.

Mitchell left the pack in the locker, gathered his new wardrobe and proceeded to the men's room.

It was after one o'clock when his cab pulled up in front of the Park Lane. It took a moment for the desk clerk to make an appearance.

"Eric Werner," said Mitchell.

The clerk was considerably overweight. Wire rimmed glasses sat low on his nose and his deliberate manner at this late hour irritated Mitchell. He fingered meticulously through his index file. "Oh, yes, Mr. Werner, here we are." He layed the key on the counter. "Suite 726 . . . if you'll just sign here."

Mitchell filled in the card and the fat man shuffled back behind the counter and reappeared a moment later with an envelope. "This was left for you."

Mitchell took the envelope.

"We also allowed a delivery of some of your personal items to be made to your room earlier."

Mitchell wondered what they would include.

In his room, he dropped the shaving kit on the bed and opened the closet door. Three obviously expensive suitcases sat side by side on the floor. They matched with the shaving kit he'd picked up in the locker at LaGuardia earlier. An attache case of similar design lay on the shelf above the clothes rod. Two suits and shirts hung from the rod. A plastic zippered bag that hung from a hook on the back of the opened door contained three pairs of shoes. Mitchell recognized everything in the closet as being quality merchandise. He opened the suitcases and ruffled through them quickly. Each contained at least one suit and two or three changes of casual clothes, all labled from L. H. van Hees, one of Munich's premier men's clothing stores. He closed the bags, returned them to the closet, lay back on the bed and opened the bulging brown envelope that the desk clerk had given him.

Inside were various objects—passport, credit cards, identification cards, driver's license—establishing his identity as Eric Werner. Mitchell looked through them carefully and found himself impressed by their authenticity. While all the items must have been recently completed, they had been made to appear appropriately worn. He removed the identification and inserted it in his wallet.

Two articles remained in the envelope. The first was a key inside a smaller envelope. A note wrapped around the key read:

Konigstrabe bus from Stuttgart airport to central bus terminal. Taxi south on Konigstrabe to Kronenstrabe, right to Lautenschlagerstrabe, left to 471 Lautenschlagerstrabe, Apartment 3.

Mitchell attached the key inside his keycase and put it back in his pocket. He folded the piece of paper once and slid it into his wallet.

The last item was an airline ticket. Mitchell opened the Lufthansa covering jacket and examined the schedule.

Flight 633 Lv NY 6:45 p
May 4, 1979 Arr Frkft 8:10 a
1/C conf Lv Frkft 9:45 a
Arr Sttgt 10:20 a

He checked the date again and it registered that he'd be leaving later the same day. He went over the schedule once more. "Six-forty-five tonight . . . hour and a half stopover in Frankfort. He slipped the ticket inside his jacket breast pocket, then removed the jacket and hung it in the closet.

It was two-thirty. Mitchell went to the window and looked down onto the street. A block away a neon light from an all-night diner blinked sporadically. Across the street, the features of Central Park hid in quiet shadows. The street was deserted. Even the streetwalkers had given up. He looked in the other direction and the scene was the same. Mitchell dropped the drape and sighed resignedly. He flipped the channels on the TV. Only one old western was on at this hour.

He sat there not moving, a slightly unsettled feeling in his stomach, that feeling that often grasps a visitor to a new city when he is alone. He silently cursed the fact it was too late for him to go out and get away from it. Still he sat, unmoving.

He watched the movie doggedly for fifteen minutes before giving up.

The day went quickly. Mitchell slept uncharacteristically late, until well past one in the afternoon, then had an extended and leisurely lunch in one of the hotel restaurants. By the time he returned to his room, it was nearly time to leave for the airport.

He arrived at JFK two hours early, checked his baggage and had a drink in the lounge.

It was an excellent flight, free of any disturbances, and attended to in an extraordinary manner by a beautiful blonde with the longest legs Mitchell had ever seen. He passed through customs without event and made his connecting flight to Stuttgart, arriving at Echterdingen

113

Airport at 10:20 a.m. as scheduled. The entire flight had taken just slightly more than eight hours, with time changes accounting for the other six.

Within an hour he had departed from the Stuttgart Central bus terminal and a cab had dropped him at 471 Lautenschlagerstrabe. It was an impressive old three-story stone building, containing only six apartments, two on each floor.

Mitchell let himself into the lobby, checked the mail box labeled "E. Werner" and removed a familiar looking brown envelope. He walked up the one flight of stairs to Apartment 3 and went inside.

It was a very nice apartment, not extravagant, yet very tastefully and comfortably done. Mitchell toured it quickly. It was completely furnished. A dresser and closet full of clothes were in the bedroom, toiletries in the bathroom, food and utensils in the kitchen, sporting goods and recreational equipment in a hall closet—completely furnished.

Mitchell lowered himself into a soft chair in the living room and opened the letter. Inside was a ticket to Munich on the German Federal Railroad. An unfamiliar handwriting in German script appeared on a note of instruction.

Reservation at Hotel Bayerischer Hof commences tonight, May 5.

"Tonight?" Mitchell protested. "Shit!"
The note continued.

Check in as representative of Hornbach Industries, Stuttgart, in conjunction with International Trade Fair. Reservation made through Trade Fair and extended for additional unspecified period of time. Take bags you've been traveling with. Leave other items here.

An identification card establishing him as an employee of Hornbach Industries was also in the envelope. Mitchell wondered if such a company existed. He placed the card in his wallet among his other I.D.'s and burned the note of instruction. The GNR railway ticket indicated a departure time of 4:30 p.m. He had hoped to get to Munich soon, but not six hours after he'd gotten off an eight hour flight. Mitchell looked at his watch. Twelve-fifteen. It had hardly been worthwhile stopping in Stuttgart. Still, he knew the purpose. If any suspicion regarding him should arise, he could be traced as someone living in Stuttgart who'd taken a train from his home to Munich. If he'd flown directly to Munich from out of country, he'd be scrutinized more closely if any problems arose.

Mitchell finished his beer and looked about the apartment again. He was certain that someone maintained a presence here, entering and leaving occasionally, for the benefit of anyone who might question a stuffed—or empty for that matter—mailbox, or an apartment where lights never burned and garbage was never thrown out. Mitchell was confident all necessary background in that regard had been adequately filled in. He collected the items he'd been carrying since New York, took a last look at the apartment and locked the door behind him.

He hailed a cab on the street and stopped at a small cafe and beer garden next to the Stuttgart Central Station. He had a very tasty helping of *maultaschen* and sat relaxing and drinking beer.

Mitchell wasn't the only one sitting alone in the garden.

In the fourth row of tables behind him, a man in a

light blue suit hummed softly to himself. He was an average sized man in his late thirties, but thinning hair and a pair of old wire-rimmed glasses added years to his appearance. Though he sat nonchalantly, behind the glasses his eyes systematically scanned the area.

His gaze stopped on David Mitchell too often to be coincidental.

The man in the blue suit didn't like beer, but he had one in front of him. Every few minutes he took a small sip and forced himself to swallow it without making a face.

His code name was Gustav Junger. He was a very precise man. He ordered beer even though he didn't like it because almost everyone else did. He had found that the observance of small details were often the factors that allowed a person to blend in with a setting. He took another sip and tried to keep his eyes from watering as he swallowed.

Junger prided himself on self-discipline. He had a will of iron, with strength and endurance to match. He occasionally denied himself certain things just to prove he could do without them. He periodically fasted for several days at a time in an attempt to discipline his body.

He looked at the man he knew only as Eric Werner and wondered if he would be able to do the job. He had serious doubts. Werner obviously wasn't a professional.

With the chiming of the clock above the central station, Mitchell made his way to the terminal and got on the train.

When Mitchell paid his tab, Gustav Junger looked at his watch. Four o'clock. Without hurrying, he hailed the waitress and settled his bill. He took one suitcase aboard the train. It was empty. He carried it for the same reason he had ordered the beer. He took a seat in the rear of the third car and settled himself comfortably. He didn't worry about where they were going. He knew. He stared intently out the window during the entire trip. But his steady gaze was not focused on the scenery outside; he had seen it many times before. It was fixed on the reflection thrown back by the double glass windows—from the front of the car—the reflection of David Mitchell.

The scenery was beautiful, and kept Mitchell awake in spite of himself. He'd forgotten what a relaxing and luxurious mode of travel the train could be. The faint, rhythmic clack of the wheels and the splendor of the scenery both lulled and transfixed him. In scarcely more than two hours the huge express covered the 225 kilometers from Stuttgart, pulled into the darkened Bahnhofplatz terminal, gave a slight shudder and stopped. Mitchell gathered his bags and stepped out the door.

He couldn't completely control the excitement which began stirring inside him as he walked below the arched sign which read: *"Herzlich Willkommen in Munchen."*

Chapter 13.

The Bayerischer Hof was truly a grand hotel. From the moment Mitchell first glimpsed the white facade through the window of his cab some two blocks away, he was favorably impressed. A personable doorman met him as the cab came to a stop at Promenadeplatz 2-6 and a smiling Bavarian bellman unloaded Mitchell's bags with professional dispatch and led him through the front door to the reception area.

The setting of the adjacent lobby was one of comfortable luxury. Groupings of sturdy orange and brown patterned chairs surrounded hard, smooth-finished tables. At least twelve huge oriental rugs covered the floor of the lobby, spaced evenly in three rows of four and separated by three or four feet of well polished parquet floor. The walls were of a light beige-orange mixture that added to the warmth of the room. More than a dozen people were seated in the lobby, which Mitchell noted, served as a lounge as well. It was a pleasant scene, different from most hotel lobbies in both decor and clientele. No one in the lobby appeared to be waiting for anything; rather, they seemed to be enjoying the relaxed atmosphere that permeated the room. Employees and

118

guests alike handled themselves with a perfect balance of aplomb and cordiality.

The clerk's question brought Mitchell's attention back to the desk. "Do you have a reservation?" The clerk's accent was unmistakably Bavarian.

"Oh, yes," replied Mitchell, fishing in his pocket. He produced a confirmation of his reservation and handed it to the clerk. "Werner," he said.

Mitchell had become so accustomed to receiving a message upon his arrival at various destinations that he was surprised when nothing awaited him at the Bayerischer Hof.

The bellman left him to his suite and Mitchell spent ten minutes in a routine security check of his quarters. He would have been surprised to find anything out of order, and as he expected, nothing was.

He unpacked the suitcases and hung the shirts, slacks and suits in the large walk-in closet near the door and put the remaining items in two drawers of the dresser.

Mitchell walked across the room and parted the pale blue drapes that covered his window. His suite was on the fifth floor of a six story hotel and afforded him a pleasant view of the boulevard below. The median that divided the east-west traffic was quite wide. Attractive assortments of colorful flowers and the manicured lush green of the grass and trees were testimony to the regularity and care of their tending. A statue of Maximilian, his back to the hotel front, faced the south. To the left, another statue of equal size stood among the trees. Several evening strollers along the boulevard sat on the steps at the base of both statues and casually surveyed the traffic that had thinned significantly from its peak an hour earlier.

It was seven-thirty. Mitchell showered and descended once again to the lobby.

The Bayerischer Hof contained sufficient facilities that one need never seek anything from outside. But Mitchell, despite the rigors of a long day's travel, was determined to see at least part of the city. It was a beautiful night, with only hints of a warm easterly breeze stirring the still air. Mitchell took advantage of the weather by having dinner at the Dachgarten, an excellent rooftop restaurant atop the Hotel Continental.

From there, Mitchell adjourned to the Hofbrauhaus for some serious drinking—and patrons of the Hofbrauhaus were indeed serious about their drinking. The immense corner building with great arched windows on the ground level and flower boxes in every window of the second floor was deceptively elegant on the outside—uproariously common on the inside. Mitchell quickly discovered there were three levels in the Hofbrauhaus and like-wise three varieties of activity. The lowest level, the Horse Pond, was decidedly lowbrow and incredibly loud. Beer and pretzels were the fare and a Bavarian band in the northeast corner of the floor added to the din. Upstairs was a restaurant of obviously higher caliber, and on the third floor, still another restaurant with a large dance band on stage.

After making a cursory inspection of each floor, Mitchell took his place amid the uproar on the lower level. Stout German women carrying a half-dozen of the huge liter steins of beer floated through the maze as gracefully as ballet dancers, never spilling a drop.

Mitchell immersed himself in the raucous atmosphere and before long had lost count of the giant liters that seemed ever present before him. He made friends with a group sitting nearby and they spent several hours singing "*In Munchen steht ein Hofbrauhaus . . .*" and other songs, all the while pounding the tabletops in an unceasing and very unrhythmic clamor. Two of them eventually passed out and another left. At one point during the night, a fight broke out across the room. It was scarcely noticed by those patrons not directly involved or knocked down in the melee. Mitchell joined onlookers in a cheer as two bullish shirt-sleeved bartenders unceremoniously threw the offenders out.

It was several hours later when Mitchell stumbled through the door and into a cab for the ride back to his hotel. He was unconscious the moment he hit the bed.

Mitchell awoke at nine the next morning, sprawled sideways across the bed. His clothes lay in a rumpled pile near the foot of the bed. He forced himself up and into the bathroom where he took two aspirin. Bleary eyed, he rummaged through the desk drawer where he'd earlier placed the small directory that listed the hotel's facilities.

The sauna was on the roof, as was the swimming pool, which Mitchell noted gratefully was nearly empty at this hour.

The extreme dry heat hit Mitchell with a blast as he opened the door and stepped into the sauna. He gasped as the hot air rushed through his mouth and nose and into his lungs. Mitchell braced himself and closed the door and took a seat on the top row, leaning back against the wall and closing his eyes. The heat was welcome now, and in fifteen minutes, Mitchell, drenched with sweat, emerged from the sauna, showered and dove into the pool for a brisk ten minute swim. So successful was this routine in reviving him that Mitchell repeated it again, and then lay back in one of the reclining wicker chairs that surrounded the pool.

The sliding glass roof was open today and Mitchell looked into a flawessly blue Munich sky. Over the southern edge of the roof, Munich's most distinctive landmark, the bulbous, cupola-topped twin towers of the Frauenkirche appeared deceptively close. The clocks on the towers indicated it was nearly one-thirty. He'd have to check at the desk for messages soon. But now, the sun was warm. He closed his eyes and settled further into the chair.

It was only a short nap—two-fifteen by the tower clocks when he awoke. Mitchell took another quick swim the length of the pool and back, then went to his room and dressed. His therapy had done a world of good. By the time he stepped off the elevator on the main floor, he had lost all recollection of his hangover.

"Any messages for 515?" Mitchell asked.

The clerk looked in the box and shook his head. *"No."*

"Are you certain?"

The clerk seemed a bit upset that he should be questioned.

"I'm expecting something," Mitchell added.

The clerk looked again, closely this time, and also checked a shelf underneath the desk where packages too large to fit in the pigeon holes were stored. "I'm sorry sir, we have nothing for you."

Mitchell was puzzled. Strange they haven't told me anything as yet, he thought.

"We'll be certain to notify you if something arrives for you."

Mitchell nodded. No point worrying about it. When they're ready, they'll let me know. "Thank you," he said to the clerk.

It was a pleasant day. Mitchell walked the short distance southeast from the Bayerischer Hof to the Marienplatz, the heart of Munich, the town square where the city hall housing Munich's municipal offices was located.

The sun shone down warmly on the square at this hour. Mitchell picked up a copy of *Suddeutsche Zeitung* from a streetside newsstand and took a seat at an attractive sidewalk cafe in the middle of the Marienplatz. He ordered lunch and drank a liter of beer as he casually looked through the paper.

The square was alive with activity. An unending variety of shops and restaurants filled the area. While the activity here was brisk and purposeful, it was not frantic. Everyone seemed able to accomplish his objectives without the pulling of hair or gnashing of teeth.

His lunch was excellent. They took the plate away and he ordered another liter and folded his paper on the table and eased himself further back into his chair.

By this time the shadow of Peterskirche, the oldest church in Munich, and another of the city's most familiar landmarks, was beginning to creep steadily across the square. Mitchell looked at the two clock faces on the three-hundred-fifteen foot tower that overlooked the Marienplatz. Nearly five o'clock.

He paid the waitress and began retracing his earlier route back to the hotel. He looked up once again at the towering Peterskirche. What a view of the square that must be, he thought. If I get a chance, I'll get up there to take a look.

At the hotel, there was still no message. The same clerk he had questioned earlier recognized Mitchell as he approached the desk and shook his head apologetically. Mitchell shrugged and continued past the desk to the lounge.

It wasn't characteristic of Mitchell to worry, yet as he thought about it, it wasn't characteristic of his contact to be out of touch with him for this long a period of time.

Mitchell brooded over it through several drinks and decided the only appropriate action under the circumstances was to forget about it until someone reminded him.

By eight-thirty Mitchell had worked his way from the lobby/lounge through two cocktail bars and a basement wine cellar that served wines from all the countries of Europe. He had settled now on a stool at the bar at Trader Vic's. He'd been surprised to find such a place in the Bayerischer Hof and if it weren't for the German language being spoken there, one might have thought he were in the Trader Vic's in Chicago's Palmer House.

On his wanderings Mitchell had been successful in getting a recommendation for an excellent seafood restaurant nearby, but had been unsuccessful on two separate attempts to get an attractive young woman to join him. Undaunted, and slightly inebriated, Mitchell went by himself. The Boettner lobster, complemented by a half-bottle of German wine, was indeed everything that had been promised.

The schedule of the last few days was beginning to catch up with Mitchell by the time he returned to the Bayerischer Hof. He stopped momentarily in the night-club on the hotel's lower level. On a normal evening Mitchell would have been geared for a long session at a place as lively as this. But under the circumstances he couldn't stay beyond one drink despite a decidedly interested glance from a lone woman sitting near him at the bar. He promised himself he'd come again.

Mitchell had undressed, turned off the light and fallen into bed before he noticed the blur that finally came into focus as a small red illuminated light on the table beside his bed. With a grunt, he reached up and switched the desk lamp on.

The red light was attached to the phone. There was a message for him in the lobby.

Mitchell suddenly felt quite sober. He dressed hurriedly and went downstairs.

"I believe I have a message—Room 515."

The clerk pulled out a brown sealed envelope. "Yes, sir. Left for you earlier this evening."

"Thank you."

In his room Mitchell sat on the bed and read the note.

Day after tomorrow. Details will follow.

He read it again, then took a match book from the table and set fire to the note. As the flames consumed it, Mitchell dropped it into the ashtray. When the last wisp of smoke had risen, he lit another match and touched it to a corner that hadn't burned. With his finger, he ground the cold ashes, then took them to the bathroom where he flushed them down the toilet.

Mitchell turned the light out once again and crawled into bed. During the past two days, he hadn't given much thought to his purpose for being in Munich. It had been a vacation thus far—the good life—well removed from normal worldly problems. But in two days, a rifle would crack and a man would die and the world would be better off without knowing it. Ironic, he thought.

He lit a cigarette and lay smoking in the dark. I hope tomorrow is a great day for you, Big Red, he thought. If I could, I'd tell you to make the most of it.

The next day was a long one for Mitchell. He began it with a sauna and swim as he had the preceding. The European Trade Fair was scheduled to begin today. Mitchell decided, that even though there was little need for it, he would absent himself from the hotel during the day lest anyone wonder why a guest who had checked in for the convention was not taken up with the day's activities. One of the desk clerks had pointed out to him that over a hundred individuals attending the convention were staying at the Bayerischer Hof even though the event itself was at the Olympia-Sporthalle, quite some distance northwest of the city's center. When the chartered bus for the Olympiapark left at eight-thirty, Mitchell was on it.

After spending an hour looking over the impressive facilities and structures of the Olympiapark, he slipped away from the rest of the group and took a cab back into the city. He spent the day browsing absently through small shops north of the city's main business section and later in the afternoon visited the Alte Pinakothek, one of the world's great art galleries.

It was after five o'clock when he returned to the Bayerischer Hof, expecting to find the more specific instruction that had been promised. Surprisingly, nothing awaited him. Under the circumstances, thought Mitchell, the only thing I can do is stay put. Tomorrow's the day, they almost have to contact me tonight.

Mitchell took up a seat in the lobby that faced the registration desk on the other end of the room. He watched with interest as a variety of people passed from the elevators or through the main door to the desk. He tried to imagine which one of the many might be his contact.

What about the thin, well-dressed young man who stood talking with one of the bellhops . . . or perhaps the fat dumpy man who stood waiting near the door in a suit which was obviously a size too small?

There was the possibility that from his vantage point now, he might well see a man handing over a familiar brown envelope to the desk attendant. If he did, of course, Mitchell would say nothing. Still, he mused, it would be interesting to know.

The waitress moved past the table again. Mitchell drained off the last half and held the bottle up slightly to attract her attention. "Please," he said, as she acknowledged him.

Around him the tables in the lobby were filling with the normal evening's complement of cocktail hour enthusiasts. The waitress brought him a beer and Mitchell took a healthy pull on it, and was in the process of lighting a cigarette when a voice at his left interrupted him.

"Excuse me," the man said, "It's a bit crowded tonight." He gestured at the occupied tables about them. "Would you mind if I join you?"

It was the fat dumpy man in the too-small suit Mitchell had seen standing near the door.

"Be my guest."

The fat man took a seat and ordered a schnapps from the waitress. Mitchell ordered another beer.

"*Prost*," the fat man said, raising his glass.

"*Prost*," said Mitchell.

From across the room, Gustav Junger slid forward in his chair. In his casual schoolteacher manner, he had been idly glancing about the lobby. With increasing frequency now, his eyes were drawn to the table occupied by Mitchell and the fat man.

Junger looked back to the pattern on his tablecloth and rearranged the position of the bottle and glass in front of him.

His mind sifted and cataloged a mental file he had committed to memory years ago, a file which required an almost constant updating.

The fat man didn't look like an agent. But that could be a strong plus for a man in this line of work.

Junger had knowledge of only two agents with physical descriptions that came close to the fat man. One was a West German whose name escaped him. But the West

German agent was older—in his mid-fifties. It irritated Junger that he couldn't think of the name.

The other was a British agent named Hill. Hill hadn't been as heavy when Junger had memorized his dossier. Nevertheless, Junger couldn't discount the possibility. Some people did not keep themselves well. Junger summoned the waitress.

Mitchell and the fat man drank without speaking. The fat man observed Mitchell carefully. They ordered another round and finally the fat man spoke.

"I knew I'd seen you before, and now I recall where," he said.

Mitchell had been trying to determine whether this man could be his contact. He waited now for him to proceed.

"It was on the bus this morning. You're here for the Trade Fair, right?"

"That's right," said Mitchell.

"I knew it," laughed the fat man. "I saw you on the bus today." He took another healthy swallow from his drink. "How'd you like the opening ceremonies?"

"Oh . . ." said Mitchell, ". . . I thought it was quite impressive."

The fat man shook his head. "I don't know . . . last year's opening was hard to top."

"I . . . uh . . . didn't have an opportunity to come last year . . . this is my first conference."

The page came out clearly over the intercom. "Mr. Hill . . . message for Mr. Hill. . ."

Gustav Junger looked over the rim of his glass at Mitchell's table. The fat man didn't flinch at the mention of the name, Hill. It took an extraordinary discipline not to react to one's name when it was called out suddenly. A good agent could do it. Junger doubted that the fat man had that kind of self-control.

Junger motioned with a finger to the waitress. The fat man continued talking about the opening ceremonies.

"That explains it," said the fat man. "Not that this wasn't nice, but I've seen so many that it's pretty hard for them to keep topping last year."

"I'm sure it is," said Mitchell. "Still, the facilities there are fabulous."

"Oh, yes," the fat man agreed. He ordered another round. Mitchell began looking for an opportunity to excuse himself.

"Too bad about the Chancellor," the fat man said.

Mitchell played along. "Yes, that was too bad."

"But I guess even though he couldn't make it today, they still expect him to speak to the group later this week."

"We'll have that to look forward to," said Mitchell.

"Say, did you see the exhibit that Badenweiler Electronics had set up?"

"Well . . . no," said Mitchell, "I'm afraid I missed that one."

"Oh, you couldn't have missed that one," said the fat man. "It was the one set up right in the center of the hall —stretched almost to the ceiling."

"Of course," Mitchell said. "I didn't recognize the name. You could hardly miss that one."

The fat man shook his head in wonder, recalling the exhibit. "I've never seen anything quite like that." He shook his head again. "Have you?" he asked. "Have you *ever* seen anything like that?"

"No," answered Mitchell sincerely. "I've *never* seen anything like that."

They drank for a precious moment in silence as the fat man recalled the remarkable exhibit and Mitchell searched for a suitable reason to leave.

Mitchell could see the fat man was about to pick up

the conversation again and Mitchell was set to change to another topic when the announcement came over the intercom. It wasn't the volume that startled Mitchell. Rather it was the impact of hearing the name in public that still somehow seemed to him as though it should be a secret.

"Mr. Werner," the clerk intoned. "Mr. Eric Werner, please call the desk."

"That's me." Mitchell felt weak at the knees when he stood.

"Don't run off," said the fat man. "Have another drink. Your message will be there a half hour from now. How important could it be, anyway?"

"I'd better check on it. You never know what might come up."

The fat man raised his glass. "See you at the conference."

Mitchell took the message to his room. Like the others, it was direct and to the point.

> Tomorrow is out. Date now uncertain,
> but realtively soon. Will be in touch.

Mitchell crumpled the note furiously and threw it against the wall. "What kind of horseshit is this?" He kicked at the wadded paper with his foot and struck the wall a resounding blow which was answered in kind from an adjacent room. Mitchell shook his head in exasperation, then sank into a chair and read the note again. When he had finished he burned it and flushed it away.

Before midnight, Gustav Junger had searched the fat man's room from top to bottom. Through an emergency phone line, he had confirmed that Robert Hill was in London on "official government business." The fat man was no more than what he appeared to be—a conventioneer from Hamburg.

It had been a long day for Junger. He had let Mitchell away from his sight in order to check on the identity of the fat man. He decided it would be a waste of time to attempt to reinstitute surveillance tonight. The plans would be finalized soon. There were many arrangements to be made. He picked up the phone in his room and dialed.

"This is Junger," he said.

At the other end Frank Walker turned up a radio in the background and began speaking. He spoke quickly and very quietly, even though there was no one else in the room. When he had finished, he hung up the phone without waiting for a reply.

Junger sat down in a chair and, as was his custom, recited the conversation verbatim in his mind. In only a moment, it had been entered indelibly upon his memory.

Chapter 14.

Mitchell decided not to think of his reason for being in Munich until someone reminded him. He crammed enough activity into the next two days to easily fill a normal week. But even though the pace he kept would seem to belie it, they were a comfortable two days.

Mitchell continued to depart the Bayerischer Hof each morning on the chartered bus for the Olympiapark. And each morning, at his first opportunity, he slipped away from the group and made his way to various parts of the city.

Taking the advice of a Hofbrauhaus bartender, Mitchell discovered the S-Bahn, Munich's metropolitan railway system, and in short order became a seasoned city traveler. Within two days, he saw everything from Munich's greatest and oldest museums to a McDonald's hamburger stand of more recent vintage. He shopped in the Luitpold Block and the Viktualienmarkt. He toured the Frauenkirche and Residenz. He strolled through the Hellabrun Zoo and through the vast Englishcher Garten Park along the Isar River.

He discovered Schwabing as the afternoon of that second day stretched on into evening. Everyone recommending it had told him, "Schwabing isn't just a district, it's a state of mind." Mitchell agreed. He wandered blissfully through the assorted pubs, beat hangouts, jazz joints, bars, and cafes that were integral parts of the international Bohemian atmosphere. Through most of the night, he was accompanied by a delightfully high-spirited art student from the University. He met her earlier in the evening and they drank and laughed their way to sun-up, ultimately finding themselves in bed in her apartment. It was with reluctance that Mitchell left quietly a few hours later as she slept.

The cab ride back to the Bayerischer Hof was a pleasant one. The morning sun had warmed things up comfortably. The city stirred to life now as the shopkeepers scrubbed the cobbled walks and washed the windows in front of their places of business. Mitchell stopped the cab a few blocks short of the hotel and had breakfast at a small cafe he had noticed on one of his earlier walks.

He was feeling quite content when he walked through the front door of the Bayerischer Hof. The envelope he noticed in the box for Room 515 jarred him suddenly back to reality.

It was after eight-thirty now, and the clerk was upset to see Mitchell still in the hotel. "Mr. Werner," he said, "you've missed the bus this morning."

"Something unexpected came up and I had to go out."

"Nothing serious, I hope."

Mitchell speculated. "Under different circumstances, it might have been."

"Is there anything we can do to help you get to the Olympiapark?"

"I'll take a cab later."

He tore open the envelope in his room. The familiar handwritten script instructed him.

* * *

Tour Peterskirche today. Spend time on the lower observation deck. A beautiful view of the Marien-platz. Particularly notice "Irmgard's." Also note a maintenance closet located along the southeastern wall of the observation deck.

The next words were set off and centered several spaces below. The capital letters hit Mitchell solidly.

TOMORROW IS THE DAY!

Mitchell crumpled the note and exhaled loudly. He unfolded the note and read it once again. He thought back several days to when he sat in the Marienplatz and thought of how excellent the view of the square must be from Peterskirche.

He destroyed the note and lay down on the bed. Irmgard's, he knew, was one of the most famous restaurants in Munich. Ceremony and formality were not high in priority there, but an unparallelled reputation for friendly service and incomparable food enabled the restaurant to host not only a steadfast crowd of regular diners, but an ever-growing number of dignitaries who visited Munich.

Someone, thought Mitchell, will apparently have his last meal there tomorrow.

Mitchell yawned widely. The night's activities were beginning to wear heavily on him. He considered what lay in store for tomorrow. He was amazed that under the circumstances, he wasn't wide-eyed with nervous anticipation, rather than unsuccessfully engaged in what now seemed to be a losing battle against sleep. His eyelids grew steadily heavier, and he rolled over finally, and closed his eyes.

* * *

He awoke at two-thirty and was having lunch in the Marienplatz at three.

Residents referred to Peterskirche affectionately as "Old Peter." It was the oldest church in Munich, mentioned more than eight-hundred years ago in the city chronicle. Mitchell didn't consider himself a connoisseur of the arts but this huge and stately old facade was imposing from the outside, magnificent on the inside. Huge arched annexes occupied the rear and both sides of the massive structure, joining at the front and center to form the main area beneath the central tower. Intricate Romanesque sculpture and objects of art adorned the interior.

Mitchell spent a moment in looking through the main floor. A winding stairway near the northern wall of the central tower appeared to lead upward to what must have been the lower observation deck. And indeed, near the base of the stairs a sign pointed out: "Lift to Observation Decks. Hours: 10 a.m.—6 p.m."

There were three stops on the elevator—Ground, Lower Deck and Upper Deck. Mitchell pushed the middle button and stepped off the elevator in a matter of seconds onto the lower observation deck. A large catwalk, perhaps eight feet in width, circled the interior of the tower. Mitchell walked first to the center and peered down to the floor of the main cathedral below. He rested his arm on a waist-high metal safety railing, firmly based in concrete, that lined the inner perimeter of the deck. He estimated the distance to the floor below at approximately a hundred feet. He turned then to the view of the Marienplatz.

The outside walls of the observation deck were solid concrete up to a three foot height. Above the wall, in large looped design, a latticework of inch-wide metal bars extended another five or six feet. The spacing in the grillwork was adequate to insure safety, yet was wide enough to offer an excellent view of the square below. Huge hinged windows that closed on the inside of the tower's ironwork were open now to allow the fresh air to enter and to accent the clarity of the view.

There were several people on the observation deck. Mitchell walked slowly around it, absorbing the view from all sides, stopping finally opposite a sign some seventy yards across the square from him. The sign read, "Irmgard's."

Irmgard's occupied a part of the second and third stories in a building that covered nearly a complete block of the Marienplatz. Because of the common frontage, the exterior of every shop along the street was identical, and Irmgard's was no more distinctive than any other business. A flower shop was on the ground floor below Irmgard's. It was not an immense establishment. Mitchell counted six sets of double windows that covered an area of perhaps eighty feet in width.

Round wooden tables sat before each pair of double windows. Mitchell could see them quite distinctly from his vantage point. Six tables fronting the windows on each floor. Twelve tables overlooking the street, and probably three times that number totally. There were few people in the restaurant at this time. Later, of course, it would be full. Every table would be taken.

From where Mitchell stood, the first set of double windows was at a slight angle to his right. Each succeeding pair further to his right increased the angle until the line to the sixth set of double windows was nearly forty-five degrees from perpendicular. Mitchell moved experimentally to several other positions along the observation deck, but none could improve upon his original spot.

A family nearby was preparing to leave. "Let's go to the upper deck now," the father said. "You can see much further over the city from there."

Mitchell glanced up to see if the interior of the tower continued unobstructed above them, but the domed ceiling of the central tower was sealed some ten feet above.

The family trooped onto the elevator to the upper level and the door closed behind them. Only Mitchell and a young couple remained on the lower deck.

Near the elevator, an open doorway led to the stairway that wound to the main floor below. The stairway appeared to have been put in when the building was originally built and it was unlikely that it got much use since the elevator had been installed. Some twenty feet beyond the elevator and stairway was another, smaller doorway, marked, "Janitorial Supplies." Mitchell glanced at the couple on the other side of the deck. They seemed oblivious to everything but themselves. Mitchell moved casually to the door and placed his hand on the knob. It was securely locked.

There was a sudden flurry of beating wings as a great flock of pigeons swooped downward from the tower above, onto the roof below the lower observation deck.

Mitchell walked once again to his vantage point and looked across to Irmgard's. He stood for several minutes staring evenly at the windows. The busboys were preparing the tables for the evening's business. Occasionally a waitress would move past a window. Mitchell focused on a chair with its back to the window. His mind's eye visualized the magnification that the scope of his M-16 rifle would provide. He could fairly see the grain of the wood on the back of the chair. He remained there, unmoving.

The elevator door opened and a group of six teenagers stepped onto the observation deck amid a mixture of laughter and conversation that broke Mitchell's concentration.

Mitchell returned his gaze across the Marienplatz one last time, then turned to the elevator and rode to the ground floor. He walked back to the Bayerischer Hof, oblivious to his surroundings. He had dinner and a drink later that evening in the hotel. He hoped to get final instructions that evening, but didn't expect it until the following morning. A nervousness stirred in the pit of his stomach and he read to change his train of thought. It wouldn't be wise to drink this evening, he decided, and after checking with the desk one last time, Mitchell went to bed at eleven o'clock. He lay there in the darkness for over two hours, unable to clear his mind of the jam of thoughts that ran repeatedly through it. Finally, after one o'clock, he fell asleep.

Mitchell bolted upright in bed as the sudden wailing of a siren shattered the quiet coolness of early morning. He ran a hand over his chest and stomach and found them wet with perspiration. The sheets were likewise damp. Mitchell sighed heavily and flopped back down onto the bed. He rolled in the sheets to dry the excess moisture from his body. He realized he'd awakened from a bad dream, and made no effort to recall it. Instead he lay for a moment in the bed, then stretched viciously and grabbed his watch from the night table. Seven-ten. He put it back and stretched and yawned again. The scream of the siren gradually abated and then faded completely in the distance.

Mitchell got up and showered and shaved and dressed. He was opening the door to his suite when he noticed the envelope that had been slid under the door. There was no question as to who it was from—it was the same kind of envelope as the others and was written in the same hand. He sat in an easy chair and opened it. As he removed the paper, two keys that had been folded inside the letter dropped onto the floor. Mitchell picked them up and looked at them for a brief moment. One was an ignition key to a Volkswagen, the other a small nondescript key that might have any one of a hundred different uses. He laid them on the end table and opened the note.

The small key is to the maintenance closet on the lower observation deck of Peterskirche. The observation deck closes at 1800 Hours. At that time, the elevator servicing the tower is shut off and the door leading to the stairway is locked. A security guard will check the area between 1800 and 1900 Hours. The janitors do not clean the area until 0800 hours the following morning.

At approximately 1500 hours, go to the lower observation deck of the Peterskirche. This will allow three hours before the deck closes. This time span should be adequate to insure that, at some point, you will be the only person there. As soon as you are alone on the deck, use the key to gain entrance to the maintenance closet. Lock it behind you. You'll find your weapon, fully loaded and complete with scope and silencer, inside a large cart against the rear wall. Also in the cart will be a one-hundred foot length of rope, a glass cutter and roll of tape.

At 2030 hours, let yourself out of the maintenance closet.

At that same time, the one security guard on duty begins checking the right hand annex on the main floor. This takes at least ten minutes. You therefore have ten minutes to perform your mission.

Attach one end of the rope to the base of the metal safety railings on the inside perimeter of the deck. Leave the balance of the rope on the floor of the deck.

Cut a four or five inch hole in one of the panes of glass covering the outside ironwork to enable you to fire without breaking the window in the tower. Use the rope to stick onto the glass, insuring that it won't accidentally fall onto the deck or out into the street.

Look across to the upper (third) floor of Irmgard's. At least two and possibly as many as six men will be seated at the table in front of the third and fourth windows from the left of the main entrance. So there can be no error, note that the third and fourth windows comprise the second set of double windows from the left. The man on the left at that table will be Big Red. Liquidate him.

It sounded so routine to Mitchell as he read it . . . an everyday occurrence. "The man on the left . . . liquidate him." He shook his head. The note continued.

Leave your weapon on the deck. Lower the rope over the inside railing to the main floor of the lobby below. Rappel down to the ground floor. Leave the rope and move quickly to the rear annex. There is a door in the right rear corner of the rear annex. Through that door are two offices used by the head of the church. The first office has a door leading outside to a small alleyway behind the church. The door unlocks from the inside and will lock behind you. A blue Volkswagen will be parked outside the door. At approximately the time you are entering the car, the guard will have discovered the rope in the tower. Since only a minute or two will have passed since the liquidation, Irmgard's will still be in a state of confusion. You should have no trouble escaping the area.

Abandon the car later at any area you see fit. Then spend a normal evening and return to the hotel as usual."

"Spend a normal evening," Mitchell mused. The note contained a few more lines.

You will spend two days in Munich after which you will be contacted at the hotel with further instructions and assistance for your departure. Do nothing until you're contacted.

There is a package for you now at the desk containing a light pair of gloves to prevent leaving any fingerprints. Also included is a flashlight, as the maintenance closet has only a small window for illumination. Use the light advisedly and with caution.

That was the end of the note. No pep talk . . . no wishes of good luck . . . as simple and uneventful as any business memorandum.

Mitchell leaned back in his chair. The feeling which had sporadically stirred inside him at intervals over the past week now churned at full force. And for the first time since he had agreed to accept the mission, Mitchell was forced to make a confession to himself.

He was afraid.

Chapter 15.

It was a very small container, so small that it fit easily into the letter box for Room 515. Inside was a small penlite flashlight and a golden-tan pair of light-weight leather gloves.

Mitchell spent a few minutes carefully wiping the two keys and the flashlight free from fingerprints and then, together with the gloves, placed them in his inside jacket pocket.

He debated with himself as to the correct method of handling the letter. He had already elected not to destroy it . . . too many details to trust to memory some twelve hours hence. He ultimately decided the safest place for it would be on his person. He folded the letter length-wise and slipped it inside his right sock, smoothing it evenly around the calf of his leg. He tested it, bending this way and that, crossing his legs, walking. In only a moment he was unaware of its presence.

The bus for the Olympiapark left at eight-thirty-five that morning. Mitchell spent a half hour in the Sporthalle looking among the various booths. By ten o'clock, he was walking through Englischer Garten.

He spent more than four hours there. It was a clear

day. The breeze that blew softly down from the mountains and through the trees and off the Isar was clean and fresh. He strolled aimlessly through the park, pausing occasionally at a park bench to feed the squirrels or simply to observe the activities of a normal spring day. Children ran noisily about, old men sat quietly in the sun, and young couples laughed together on the grass. Anyone noticing Mitchell probably thought him preoccupied. Contrarily, he was unaware of any particular thoughts. He was simply marking time.

He had lunch in the busy outdoor Cafe Seehaus on a patio overlooking a quiet lake in the park. He sat there for a full hour after he had finished his lunch, smoking a cigar and watching a handful of small rowboats crisscrossing at random on the lake's glassy surface. When he looked at his watch, it was shortly after two o'clock. Mitchell summoned the waitress, paid his bill and left.

It was three-ten when he walked through the front door of Peterskirche. Mitchell double checked his watch against the tower clocks, then went directly to the elevator and rode to the lower observation deck.

There were six people on the deck when Mitchell stepped off.

He wandered slowly arond the deck, pretending to study the view. As others would occasionally work their way around the tower to the proximity of where he was standing, he moved off unobtrusively to avoid direct personal contact.

A mother and father with their small daughter left a few minutes after Mitchell arrived, leaving only one couple and an old man on the observation deck.

Mitchell lingered momentarily opposite the sign for Irmgard's. His eyes focused on the second set of double windows . . . the third and fourth windows respectively from the main entrance at the left. The table sat exactly in the middle. Mitchell satisfied himself that the angle of fire to the target would not be so severe as to cause difficulty.

The elevator door opened and another couple joined the man and woman who had been there since Mitchell arrived. They greeted one another warmly and the couple who had been there first indicated the most notable points of interest to the new arrivals. After a few minutes the four of them departed.

Only Mitchell and the old man remained. He was a very old man, slightly stooped, with a long white beard and thick white hair that stuck out from the underneath a worn and faded hat. He wore an overcoat, though the day was decidedly warm. The coat was too big for him. He stood in one spot on the deck staring into the distance and puffing occasionally from a hand-carved pipe that was clenched firmly between his teeth.

Mitchell was a third of the way around the deck from the old man and he glanced impatiently at his watch. It was after four already and the nervousness in Mitchell's stomach was stirring again despite himself.

He hadn't been aware that the old man had noticed him, and when he spoke out, it surprised Mitchell.

"Are you still there?" The old man was looking vaguely in Mitchell's direction.

Mitchell didn't hear exactly what it was that the old man said. He thought he may have been talking to himself. "Pardon me," Mitchell said. "Were you talking to me?"

The old man shifted his gaze now directly upon Mitchell. "Yes, I was," he laughed. "I'm afraid I must apologize a bit. I thought I wasn't alone up here, but wasn't quite certain. I'm blind, you see."

The tension caused by Mitchell's fear of a direct encounter with someone who might later be a witness abated. "No need to apologize," said Mitchell. "I didn't realize. . ."

The old man dismissed it with a laugh and a wave of his hand. "Well, I guess an observation deck is not one of the most likely places to find a blind man."

"No, it isn't," Mitchell agreed.

The old man made no effort to move closer and Mitchell maintained his position.

"No," the old man repeated, "not the most likely place." He looked again in the direction of the square and then back toward Mitchell. "Would you like to know why I come here?"

Mitchell looked at his watch and didn't really give a damn why the old man came there. "If you'd like to tell me," he said.

"As a young man, I came here often. My memories of this place are so vivid, that when I stand here and smell the air and hear the noises in the square. I can actually see it all again."

Mitchell didn't reply.

"I suppose this sounds like an old man's foolishness to you."

"No, it doesn't," said Mitchell after a moment. He looked across to Irmgard's. "I'm certain that as long as I live, I'll never forget the view from this spot."

They stood without speaking for several moments. Four young schoolgirls started briefly from the elevator for a moment, but then realizing they were only on the lower deck, scrambled back into the elevator for the ride to the top.

"I've always thought the view was prettier from the lower deck rather than the higher," said the old man, "because you're closer here to the thing that really brings the picture alive—the people. They're real from here . . . not tiny dolls without character or dimension.

You can see them smile from here, and laugh from here, and argue from here, and curse from here."

And sometimes, thought Mitchell, you might see them die from here.

The old man drew his coat closer about his shoulders. "It feels as though it may rain soon . . . as if a cloud has passed over."

Mitchell looked out over the square. Though he hadn't noticed it previously, what had been a sunny afternoon was now being threatened by an ominously growing cloud bank to the northwest. "You may be right," he said. He looked at his watch again. "Probably a good idea to leave now and beat the rain."

The old man continued to stare diligently into the distance. "The rain doesn't bother me," he said. "Why should an old man of my age worry about getting a little wet? I haven't reached this age without surviving much more than that."

"And you haven't survived this long without using common sense either."

The old man seemed determined to stay.

"Well, it *is* getting late," Mitchell said. "I have an appointment that I have to keep." He walked to the elevator door and pushed the button. In a moment the elevator door opened.

"*Auf Wiedersehen,*" said the old man. "I've enjoyed visiting with you."

"*Auf Wiedersehen,*" Mitchell said.

Mitchell shuffled his feet as if walking but remained outside the elevator. The door closed and the empty elevator began its descent. Mitchell quietly and painstakingly moved along the wall some ten yards from the elevator and waited.

The old man remained at the same spot. Within a few minutes the first heavy drops of rain hit the roof below the lower deck.

It was nearly five o'clock. Mitchell stood motionless and considered what action to take. He had been lucky in that no one else had come to the lower deck within the last hour. He was about to risk unlocking the maintenance closet even though the old man was still there. He was reaching for the key when the old voice spoke abruptly.

"Young men have appointments they must keep . . . old men have time they must pass." The old man muttered to himself, shuffling to the elevator, his hand sliding gently along the inside rail. He pushed the "Down" button and waited as the elevator motor engaged above and began its descent from the upper deck.

Mitchell stood scarcely breathing as the door to the elevator opened. The old man stopped for a moment before entering the elevator and Mitchell's hair raised on the back of his neck as the old man looked blankly in his direction. He held the questioning gaze for a moment, straining to hear, but as the door to the elevator began to close, the old man grunted and hurried into the elevator.

Mitchell thrust a perspiring hand inside his jacket and quickly put on the leather gloves he'd carried since early morning. He wiped the door knob briskly to remove any fingerprints he might have left when he tried the door on the previous day. It took only a moment for him to get the key and let himself into the maintenance closet. Once inside, he locked the door behind him.

Mitchell stood for a moment and allowed his eyes to adjust to the dim indirect light that shone through a very small window three-quarters of the way up the wall opposite the doorway. The closet was a small area in width, drab in its concrete construction, with an extremely high ceiling of some ten feet. An unpleasant musty odor filled the room. A variety of common janitorial supplies were scattered at random about the interior and Mitchell stepped cautiously as he worked his way among the brooms, mops and buckets to the large wheeled cart against the far wall. A worn and dusty tarpaulin was thrown over the top of the cart. Mitchell lifted the corner and peered inside.

It was difficult to distinguish the black barrel and stock, laying in the dark shadows at the bottom of the cart. For a moment, Mitchell didn't believe it was there. He leaned over the edge and worked his hand gently across the bottom. He had scarcely began moving it before his fingers brushed the coldness of metal and he closed them around the unmistakably familiar features of the weapon he knew so well.

He removed the rifle from the cart with one hand and with the other, turned a nearby mop bucket upside down and positioned it against the wall beneath the window. It was five-twenty. He sat down on the bucket and rested his back against the wall. He held the rifle on his lap and waited.

In the semi-darkness, he sat unmoving, and the passage of time for the whole world seemed to Mitchell to be suspended in that small dank room. He denied himself the satisfaction of checking his watch and with a great effort was able to keep his mind clear.

Outside the steady force of the rain increased. The monotonous patter on the roof seemed to accent the reluctance of the passing time.

The sudden rattling of the door handle came without warning and startled Mitchell to the extent that he nearly dropped his weapon. He pulled the M-16 firmly to his shoulder and his hand went instinctively to the bolt. His heart pounded inside him with what was a wildly familiar combination of fear and excitement. It was a feeling he recognized from years past. And as he hated it, he also loved it. Every sense was operating on its keenest edge. Had he been heard?

In an instant, the handle rattled once more and the security guard, satisfied that all was in order on the lower observation deck, locked the door to the stairway and took the elevator to the ground floor.

Mitchell sat for several minutes breathing heavily, the barrel of his weapon pointed at the door. He relaxed gradually, and looked at his watch. It was six-thirty. The light entering the small east window of the maintenance closet was dimmer now as the sun was sinking lower behind the buildings on the west side of the Marienplatz.

Leaning his weapon carefully in the corner, Mitchell pulled his pants leg up and slid the letter out. He stood to get closer to the source of light above his head and read it over several times and then replaced it. Moving again to the cart, Mitchell folded the tarpaulin further back. Coiled at the bottom was a great length of rope which he carefully removed and set near the doorway. He tested it for strength and found it to be of very high quality nylon. It was relatively narrow, making it less bulky and easier to handle, but it was obviously strong enough to support his weight.

Mitchell returned to the cart. Removing his penlite from his pants' pocket, he located the roll of tape and the glasscutter in a corner on the bottom. He turned the light out and put all the items in his jacket pocket.

He sat down once again on the bucket and picked the rifle up. He pointed it toward the door and peered through the scope and down the barrel. The near absence of light prevented him from sighting adequately. He ran his gloved fingers across the magazine and bolt, down to the silencer on the end of the barrel. He set the weapon back in the corner.

He wanted to have a smoke, but knew he couldn't risk

it. He took the glasscutter from his pocket and played with it for a moment, then put it away and looked back at his weapon.

I hope to hell this thing is still zeroed the way I had it in Colorado, he thought. A hell of a long way to bring something and then not have an opportunity to double check it for accuracy. He remembered when he'd been in basic training and somehow the tip on his sight had been accidently tapped a fraction of an inch to the right by the people who had the responsibility of locking the weapons up after every firing session. Only a fraction of an inch . . . but what was a fraction of an inch at a few feet, became a few feet at a hundred meters! He'd almost failed to qualify on the M-14 because of it. What if this weapon had been jarred ever-so-slightly while enroute from Colorado?

Mitchell found himself beginning to worry and it irked him. After all, he thought, this outfit isn't exactly a bunch of rookies! They know what they're doing. They know it has to be perfectly zeroed. It *will* be!

He convinced himself.

The rain continued. It had been falling for so long it hadn't occurred to him that it might have an effect. Christ, he thought, what if it's raining so hard that my vision's impaired? He considered it a moment, but saw the direction his thoughts were once again taking and forced it from his mind. He had taught himself years ago that worrying about things rarely changed the outcome. That would be particularly true on this night.

It was after seven o'clock. Less than an hour and a half.

He leaned back against the wall and listened to the rain and thought about the girl art student he'd met in Schwabing.

At eight-twenty it was dark. The rain had gradually

subsided to a drizzle and finally stopped altogether. Mitchell took the note once again from inside his sock, and placing it in the cart under the tarpaulin, turned on the penlite and studied it for the final time. The light coming through the small window was minimal now, but Mitchell was accustomed to the darkness and after allowing a moment for his eyes to readjust from the glare of the penlite, he replaced the paper in his pocket, picked up his weapon and walked to the door.

Eight-twenty-five. Mitchell felt inside his pocket for the glasscutter. He placed it in his right hand jacket pocket, the tape in his left hand jacket pocket and all other items in his pants pocket.

Eight-twenty-seven. As quietly as possible, Mitchell pulled back the bolt of the M-16. Even in the dim light, he caught sight of an instantaneous flicker as the brass casing slipped into place and the bolt slammed forward. It was a loud noise—decidedly louder than Mitchell would have liked, but nonetheless necessary to lock the weapon properly. He was certain the sound did not travel beyond the small room. With his thumb, he pushed the safety off.

Eight-twenty-nine. Mitchell took several deep breaths to steady himself, picked the coil of rope from the floor and threw it over his left shoulder. He took the key to the door and slipped it carefully into the lock.

It was exactly eight-thirty as Mitchell turned the key in the lock of the maintenance closet. He locked the door behind him and hurried to the outer edge of the observation deck where he stood his weapon against the wall.

There were no lights in the observation deck, but lights from the Marienplatz below reflected brilliantly off the wet pavement. Together with the lights from the main floor of the cathedral, Mitchell had no problem finding his way about.

He tied one end of the length of rope to the base of the iron railings. No sounds could be heard from the floor below.

Pulling the tape from his pocket, Mitchell measured off approximately a foot. He stuck both ends of the tape securely to the glass at shoulder height in the spot he had predetermined, leaving a loop of several inches in the middle which he grasped firmly in his left hand. With his right hand, Mitchell cut a circle of approximately six inches with the glasscutter. As he completed the full circle, he lifted the piece from the window using the tape handle and laid it on the floor. Then he picked up the rifle, and for the first time, looked through the opening across the street to Irmgard's.

The sounds of the square were more distinct now, and as Mitchell gathered the rifle firmly into place, laying his cheek along the cool stock and sighting through the scope, the magnified detail of the dining room across the square jumped abruptly into view. He could fairly hear the laughter and conversation, mixed with the clacking of dishes and the scraping of silver as busboys cleared vacated tables and arranged new place settings.

He sighted on the second set of double windows. There were two men at the table, yet now, only a portion of one—the man on the left—filled the scope.

He adjusted the weapon slightly and the thin crosshairs came to rest behind the tip of the man's right ear. He was speaking now and Mitchell could see the movement of his facial muscles. The angle was such that Mitchell sighted down on, and behind, his ear; the other features of the face were indiscernible except for brief instances when he glanced to his right. Mitchell noted an involuntary twitch . . . a nervous tic in the right eye as the face was turned.

The crosshairs were fixed now. Mitchell began the

steady increase in pressure on the trigger which could have only one inevitable conclusion.

It was in that fraction of a second when the face turned once again to the right—a bit further this time than before—that the fleeting glimpse of recognition flashed through Mitchell's mind.

It was in that fraction of a second that Mitchell recognized the face that filled the scope.

It was in that fraction of a second that the resistance of the trigger which had built to the brink of destruction suddenly spent itself and the finger applying the pressure found no opposition an. flew freely backward where it rested now at the rear of the trigger guard.

It was in that fraction of a second that a pane of glass in the second set of double windows on Irmgard's third floor disintegrated, spewing minute crystaline fragments in its wake.

And it was in that fraction of a second that the skull of the man on the left was shattered by the force of a bullet from a high-powered rifle that literally raised him from his seat and flung him across the corner of the table into a lifeless mass on the floor beyond.

Mitchell lowered the scope, a look of bewildered horror on his face. It was impossible! He grabbed the rifle and sighted the scope across the street once again.

"Oh, my God!" He was numbed as the scope verified what he knew he had seen.

Lying dead on the floor, amidst bits of brain and bone and flesh and blood, was Karl Stehlin, Chancellor of West Germany.

Chapter 16.

Mitchell stood with his mouth open, staring in disbelief across the square. A great outrageous confusion tore at his innards and bombarded his mind. In his distraction, the weapon slipped from his hands and it was only by luck that he grasped instinctively and caught hold of it before it could clatter noisily on the floor of the observation deck.

The quick movement served to clear his mind. Mitchell realized he had only a few moments to escape before the guard on the main floor returned from his inspection of the right annex. He laid the weapon on the floor, and with his other hand grabbed the heavy length of coiled rope which was tied to the base of the inside railing and dropped it through the rails toward the floor of the cathedral below.

The rope jerked violently as it reached its end some three feet above the floor and continued to twitch spasmodically as Mitchell hurriedly descended. He dropped the last several feet in his haste, and scrambling quickly, with a glance over his shoulder, ran through the deserted rear annex. The sound of his footsteps seemed to echo deafeningly off the walls and arched ceiling. He expected to hear someone yell for him to stop, or to feel a bullet slam between his shoulder blades.

In only a moment he was at the door in the rear of the annex. He found the first office and without stopping to see whether the guard had yet discovered the rope, he opened the door to the outside and leapt into the alleyway. As promised, a blue Volkswagen sat outside the back door. Mitchell had the key in his hand and in a matter of seconds had pulled down the alley and onto a main street that would carry him far from the Marienplatz.

Less than four minutes had elapsed since Karl Stehlin had passed to eternity. On the third floor of Irmgard's, the confusion of the moment had changed to frightened chaos.

At six minutes after Karl Stehlin's last breath, a puzzled security guard in the Peterskirche stood staring up dumbly at a rope which dangled from the lower observation deck.

Across the street, the atmosphere turned to one of stunned silence as people realized what had happened. The Chancellor's security detail, who at his request, had been dining in an adjoining room, were on the scene. While two of them acted to control the crowd, four others rushed to the windows and systematically scanned the buildings across the square. Normally two of them would tend personally to the Chancellor in an emergency situation, but a quick glance in his direction indicated the futility of any effort in that regard.

They were an efficient group. It had been only at the Chancellor's insistance that they dined in another room, and even then, with reluctance and many professional misgivings.

At this precise moment they were collectively cursing the days they were born.

Within ten minutes they had sealed off the entire Marienplatz and with the cooperation of the police, had begun a search of the buildings immediately across the square from Irmgard's.

In those ten minutes, David Mitchell had driven to a busy parking lot in Schwabing where he left the blue Volkswagen, and inside it, everything he had used to carry out his mission. He burned the note with his instructions, scattering the ashes in the street, and caught a cab to the Hofbrauhaus. By the time the Chancellor's security detail was standing over the M-16 on the lower observation deck of Peterskirche, Mitchell was finishing his second liter of beer.

It was twenty minutes after nine when the Bavarian band stopped suddenly in the middle of a number. The cat calls and obscenities that could be expected from the crowd were short-lived however, as a somber-looking man with a high pitched voice spoke into the PA system. "Karl Stehlin is dead!" he said. There was an audible gasp, then cries of protest and disbelief. The man at the PA system repeated what he had said. "He was assassinated within the past hour as he dined at Irmgard's. His assassin has not been apprehended."

The man with the high voice turned off the PA system and walked off the platform.

After a brief consultation, the band disassembled their instruments and left. Within a few minutes, about half the patrons had departed. The balance, which included Mitchell, clustered around the TV set at the bar, drinking in wide-eyed disbelief and talking of what had happened in incredulous tones.

Mitchell was perhaps more shocked and sickened than anyone. An hour later, his mind was still a cluttered mass of perplexities that he had been unable to sort out and evaluate. What happened? And why? Something was terribly wrong!

He took a cab to the Bayerischer Hof, where he walked through the uncommonly silent and nearly empty lobby to the elevator that took him to the fifth floor. Once inside his room, Mitchell didn't bother with a light, but only switched on the TV and slumped into a chair and sat there in a daze in the darkness.

The TV was showing only the repetition of things he had seen earlier. "No further developments," they said.

Mitchell scarcely noticed the set as he wrestled with his thoughts in an effort to analyze just what had happened. Eventually, he managed to regain sufficient composure to consider it objectively.

As he saw it, there were three possible explanations.

The first was that the wrong man had been killed. Mitchell thought back to his training as he considered it.

"Who is Big Red?" Mitchell had asked Walker.

"Doesn't make any difference, Eric. You wouldn't know him anyway," Walter had replied.

That didn't fit. Maybe the wrong man *had* been killed. This had been Mitchell's first thought from the moment he recognized the face in the scope. By some gross chance happening, the Chancellor of West Germany had been shot by mistake. Perhaps he had counted wrong when he counted the sets of double windows. It could have happened. Irmgard's Restaurant occupied space within a huge building that housed many other businesses. It was possible that he began counting from the wrong point.

But Mitchell didn't believe it.

Perhaps his contact had made a mistake . . . given Mitchell a wrong floor . . . or wrong window . . . or wrong position at the table. Mitchell had wondered when he first read the note how they could be so certain that someone would be sitting at that given point at that given time. What if the target had been seated at another table ... or sat in a different chair ... or gotten sick ... or gone to the john?

The TV set flickered in the darkness, sending alternate shadows and spears of light across the creases knit on Mitchell's brow. He shook his head. He didn't believe his contact had made a mistake. Everything connected with the mission had gone too smoothly to think that the one most important thing would be blown.

There was also the fact that the first postponement and rescheduling of the mission coincided with the postponement and rescheduling of the Chancellor's visit to Munich.

Finally, it seemed to strain credibility to think that in a politically motivated assassination attempt, the death of a figure such as the Chancellor of West Germany could be a wild coincidence.

There was a second possible explanation—one that Mitchell wanted to believe—that Karl Stehlin was in fact "Big Red." If so, he *had* been the designated target and the mision had been successful.

Three hours ago, Mitchell had nearly convinced himself it was true.

But Karl Stehlin had been the most respected man in West Germany. His character and reputation were above reproach and had never been tarnished in a profession that traditionally drew the closest possible public scrutiny. He was the most influential man in West Germany and a leader in politics on a worldwide scale. He wasn't a man who needed to seek power; he already possessed it.

Mitchell didn't want to recognize the third possibility.

In fact, he'd refused at first to admit it might have happened. But over the past several hours the nagging unrest from unanswered questions continued to gnaw at him. When considered individually, they had been random bits of seemingly insignificant information. Only when they were evaluated together did they point to another conclusion.

Mitchell touched a match to a cigarette and a thick shroud of smoke rose between him and the screen. He tried to piece together exactly what was bothering him. He thought back to his first contact regarding the mission and worked his way to the present. There were a handful of things he'd forgotten or not noticed or dismissed when they originally happened that seemed unusual to him in retrospect.

There was the first letter he received that began the whole affair. Distribution had been to the President of the United States, Mitchell, and the project file which Walker controlled. Obviously distribution on such a sensitive item would be limited. Yet the letter came from the personnel office of the Army Intelligence and Security branch and bore the standard letterhead of the Officer in Charge. Why involve him? No practical reason, Mitchell told himself—except it made the letter appear official.

Then a few weeks later at the Federal Building—the security guard. Certainly not a run-of-the-mill part-time worker. He had been sharp and meticulous in his dress and manner. He had a bearing about him that wasn't consistent with what you normally find in a man in that position. No, he was definitely not a normal security guard.

Mitchell pondered another point. He'd never seen or heard of a classification marking like the one that covered the orders of the mission. That didn't mean it couldn't exist, but Mitchell had spent a lot of time with sensitive documents and had never seen anything classified in that manner.

And why use an M-16? Of course, anyone could get one; but still, it was an American weapon. And why leave it and everything else behind? Granted, it had been easier to escape without having to worry about getting everything out, but it certainly wouldn't have been impossible to do and it would have made the subsequent investigation more difficult.

Mitchell's head ached and he rubbed the palm of his hand across his forehead.

He'd met only one man connected with the mission— Walker. He had been paid in cash to a foreign bank. He had no records or knowledge to indicate the name of his organization. He didn't know where it was located, or how many were in it. He *did* have a phone number but he'd been told to use it only if he received specific instructions to do so. And at this hour, and under these circumstances, a long distance call to the United States would be foolish to say the least.

Mitchell sat bleary-eyed in the darkness in Munich. He reviewed everything a half-dozen more times. And finally, when he was convinced the answers were always going to turn up the same, Mitchell admitted to himself what he had harbored in the back of his mind for several hours. It wasn't easy to face. But considering everything, it was the most likely of all the possibilities.

He thought for a moment he would be sick to his stomach.

He had been duped into assassinating the Chancellor of West Germany.

Chapter 17.

The past twenty-four hours had seemed a lifetime to Mitchell, and the previous night, one that might never end. He finally nodded off fitfully in the hours of early morning and when he awakened with a sudden jerk, he found himself still slumped in the chair.

With consciousness, a hope that he'd dreamt the entire situation welled up within him. But the feeling of relief he ached for disintegrated as quickly as it had grown when the still-operating TV set ran yet another repetition of the events of the preceding night.

Mitchell rose awkwardly from the chair, stretched and massaged the stiffness from his neck. He turned the TV set off and went to the bed and lay down fully clothed atop the covers. He drew his knees up and turned on his side. It was eight o'clock and bright sunlight filled the room. He knew he must have more sleep if he expected to analyze his position objectively and somehow, after fifteen minutes of blank, wide-eyed staring into the patterned wall, he cleared his mind and dropped off to sleep.

Four hours later Mitchell awoke. The confusion that had plagued him since the assassination was not as overwhelming now. As the cool water from the shower ran soothingly through his hair and down his forehead he was able to consider less subjectively which course of action he should take.

He dressed and went to the lobby. The newspaper vending machines outside the door of the hotel were empty and a short old man attending to them raised his arms in a helpless gesture. "Can't keep enough on hand. They've made three extra runs this morning."

Mitchell went back into the hotel. In the lobby, as on the street outside, activity was nearly at a standstill. Those who spoke did so in hushed and reverent tones befitting the solemnity of the day.

"Do you know where I might find a paper?" Mitchell asked the clerk.

"We bought a large number of extra copies this morning," the clerk said, producing a copy of *Suddeutsche Zeitung* from a pile stacked on the floor behind the counter.

"STEHLIN MURDERED!" the headline screamed. The caption appeared over a photo of Karl Stehlin and together they occupied half the front page.

Mitchell looked at the headline again, the expression on his face mirroring his disgust with what he saw. The word "murdered" bothered him. It was ugly and he hadn't expected it to be used.

The clerk noted his look of fixed concern. "A tragedy, wasn't it?"

Mitchell pulled his attention from the paper. "Yes," he nodded. "A horrible tragedy."

"Probably the work of someone who had no idea what he was actually doing."

"Yes," he said. "It may well have been someone who had no idea what he was doing."

Mitchell turned and walked to the elevators.

* * *

Mitchell opened wide the window to his room and the cool and fragrant air that rushed in comforted him. He took one of the easy chairs and slid it in front of the window and, propping his feet on the sill, sat there for several minutes with his eyes closed as the vacillating breeze billowed the curtain and tousled his hair.

The time that had passed since the previous night had done much to aid Mitchell in evaluating his predicament. Though by no means did he have all the answers he wanted, he at least found himself able to judge things on a more rational basis than he had found possible the past night.

Even in the light of morning however, he still agreed with the ultimate premise he had reached last night, namely, that he'd been duped into killing Karl Stehlin. The next step was to determine what to do about it. As he reviewed it, it was obvious that this also wouldn't be a problem with an easy solution.

His original orders called for him to stay two more days in Munich, at which time he'd supposedly receive final instructions along with transportation out of Germany.

But, of course, if he'd been used as a pawn, he couldn't rely on that happening. As he thought of it now, it seemed foolish to attempt to arrange transportation out of the country so shortly after the assassination. Surely the German police would have extraordinary security at travel terminals.

That the idea was a bad one probably made no difference. The likelihood he'd be contacted at all seemed remote now.

Of course, there was one other unpleasant thought that couldn't be ignored. For the record, Dave Mitchell was officially dead. If any man had ever become completely expendable, Mitchell was it.

Mitchell opened his eyes and snapped the paper open in front of him. "STEHLIN MURDERED!" The headline leapt off the page.

The paper was substantially larger than the normal issue and was almost entirely devoted to news of the assassination and biographical sketches of the deceased Chancellor.

Mitchell read the stories carefully. Most of the details of the assassination had been pieced together. The investigators still hadn't been able to determine how access to the lower observation deck had been gained, but it was possible that someone had hidden in the janitorial closet on the lower observation deck of the Peterskirche until the building had closed. A section of glass was removed from an outside window and the Chancellor was assassinated. The assassin had then lowered himself by rope to the floor of Peterskirche and escaped through an outside door, probably in the rear annex.

"Unfortunately," the paper reported, "no one was seen fleeing Peterskirche after the assassination."

The German Secret Service was asking anyone who had visited the lower observation deck of Peterskirche within the last few days and had seen anything unusual or suspicious to come forward with the information. No leads had developed as yet from that request.

Was it true an American M-16 rifle had been the death weapon?

"Yes," a German official was quoted as saying. "An M-16 specifically equipped with scope and silencer for such an assassination. But," he was quick to point out, "the fact it was an American weapon has no bearing on the case. Anyone who commits a professional assassination such as this can obtain any type of weapon in the world for his purpose."

The investigators would suggest no theory relating to who the assassin was or why the act had been committed.

Mitchell turned the pages in search of any more specific information the Secret Service or police might have discovered. Apparently, there was none. As yet, it appeared they still hadn't found the blue Volkswagen in Schwabing.

It was after two thorough readings of the paper, while he was paging through it for the third time, that Mitchell's eye was drawn to a small item on the inside column of page nineteen. It didn't relate to the assassination and that was probably why he hadn't noticed it on his first readings. In fact, he had passed over it for the third time, scanning what seemed a relatively insignificant paragraph and going on to the next page before what he had seen registered within his subconscious and pulled his gaze back.

FIRE CLAIMS LIFE OF MUNICH MAN

A faulty gas line has been listed as the cause of an early morning fire which claimed one life and totally destroyed a Menzing two-flat. According to neighbors, the structure burst into flame shortly after midnight and was totally engulfed when firemen arrived on the scene. The only occupant, burned beyond recognition, was subsequently identified through dental records as Gustav Junger, 32.

Mitchell stared fixedly at the name.

Its significance did not come to him quickly. Something hauntingly familiar about it lurked in the recesses of his mind and prevented him from passing over it. It was after a half hour of probing thought that he remembered something Walker had told him. "There's really no need for you to know," Walker had said, "but in case something comes up later, and for some reason you *have* to know . . . your contact's name is Gus."

He thought further back to the cabin in the Colorado Rockies to the night he'd heard Walker on the telephone asking how "Younger" was doing.

Younger . . . Junger. Gustav Junger!

It took Mitchell less than a minute to make up his mind. His contact, Gustav Junger, was dead. If Mitchell remained here, it was only a matter of time until someone came for him. If he waited around for a "ticket", he was certain it would turn out to be a one-way ticket to eternity.

Mitchell packed in ten minutes. In fifteen minutes, he was checking out at the front desk of the Bayerischer Hof.

The hotel staff, under these circumstances, could have been mistaken for employees of a funeral parlor. They spoke in exaggerated low tones and moved with measured care to the point that it irritated Mitchell.

"Where would you like your mail forwarded, Mr. Werner?" the clerk whispered.

"I don't expect any mail to arrive," said Mitchell. His normal speaking voice sounded like a shout across the subdued lobby. "If I should get any, forward it to my home address."

He paid his bill and a bellhop carried his bags to the curb. The doorman hailed a cab.

"Airport," Mitchell said as he jumped in.

The cab driver wanted to talk about what had happened. Mitchell had other things on his mind.

"A hell of a thing when someone can kill the Chancellor and leave everything behind him and still not leave a clue to who he was or why he did it," the driver offered.

"A hell of a thing."

"Probably Communists."

Through the rear view mirror Mitchell watched as a green Porsche made a turn a half-block behind them.

"It's enough to shake you up," the driver continued.

"If you don't mind, I'd rather not talk about it."

The driver was offended and grudgingly turned his full attention back to the wheel. The cab braked to a stop at a red light and Mitchell caught sight of a small restaurant mid-way down the block to his left.

"Turn left here, will you? I want to pick up a pack of cigarettes at that cafe."

He closed the door without looking back and went into the cafe. Within a few minutes he stepped back into the street, stopping momentarily to light a cigarette. Over the edge of the cupped hands that sheltered his match, Mitchell saw the green Porsche. It sat on the opposite side of the street at the end of the block.

Gustav Junger waited patiently in the Porsche while Mitchell went into the cafe. An unusual stop. Perhaps he had discovered he was being tailed. Did he look Junger's way when he lit the cigarette?

Mitchell flipped the match into the air with his middle finger and climbed back into the cab. Only one person in the Porsche.

They continued to the airport and as Mitchell could occasionally determine from glimpses in the mirror, the green Porsche did so, too.

It was something Mitchell had expected would happen. He had no plans to fly out of Munich on the day after an event like that which had occurred the previous night. The terminal, he was certain, would be virtually crawling with police and secret service men checking every departure from the city that looked the least bit suspicious. The same would be true of rail and bus terminals.

Mitchell was confident he could get through a police check if he had no alternative. His cover, regardless of what had happened, was excellent. Still, he had no desire to press his luck.

Junger realized now that they were going to the airport, which upset him. Werner was becoming irrational. There was no telling what he might do now. "That's what happens when you use amateurs," Junger said aloud. He felt inside his jacket and closed his hand on the snub-nosed pistol under his left armpit. He had been told only to keep Werner under observation. But in the field, you sometimes had to make decisions in order to adapt to a changing situation.

If Werner tried to get on the plane, Junger might have to prevent it. He shook his head in disappointment. Werner wasn't handling this very well.

Mitchell had gone to the airport for two reasons. One was to determine whether anyone was following him. The other was to leave his baggage behind. In checking out of the Bayerischer Hof, Mitchell took his bags to avoid suspicion. The luggage, however, certainly wasn't conducive to the rapid and light travel that he would find necessary to elude the occupant of the green Porsche—and any others who might have an interest in his whereabouts.

As he paid the cab driver outside the internatioal terminal he saw the Porsche park some distance further back. It was too far to make out faces, but Mitchell could see that a man in a white sweater left the car and entered the terminal near the Air France counter at the opposite end from where Mitchell stood.

Mitchell rented a large locker and placed his luggage

inside. Then he went back to the terminal entrance near where the green Porsche was parked. Mitchell could see by a sign across the street that the car was in a passenger loading zone. Parking in excess of fifteen minutes was prohibited. The man in the white sweater wasn't in sight.

A bank of telephone booths near the door caught Mitchell's attention. Walking to a booth, he scanned the phone book listings and dialed a number.

"Zern's Towing," the voice at the other end of the line answered.

"There's a green Porsche in front of the Air France counter in the international terminal of the airport," said Mitchell. "It quit on me and I'm late for a very urgent meeting, so I'm going to have to leave it here and take a cab. I'd like you to tow the car to my residence and my wife will pay you there for the tow."

Mitchell gave the license number and a ficticious name and address. "Get here as soon as possible," he said. "I don't want the car sitting here so long that someone vandalizes it."

Zern's Towing assured him they would be there within fifteen minutes.

Mitchell took a seat in the terminal and waited.

It was in fact, only twelve minutes later when the huge red tow truck, greatly in need of paint, pulled up beside the green Porsche in front of the international terminal. An efficient man was handling the rig. He had set the chains and was nearly ready to lift the car on the hooks when the man in the white sweater, apparently just catching sight of what was taking place, rushed out to his car.

The tow truck had caught Junger off guard. He reacted instinctively, but had taken only a half dozen steps outside the terminal when he realized that he may not have given Eric Werner enough credit.

He spun on his heel and pushed back through the crowd.

Mitchell had taken advantage of the moment to pass from the international to the domestic terminal. For a few frantic moments, Junger scoured the terminal. Mitchell wasn't to be seen.

Junger regained his composure and walked back cooly to explain the misunderstanding to Zern's Towing. It would be a little more difficult now, he admitted. He smiled to himself. He liked a challenge.

Mitchell was in a cab, bound once again for Munich. For over an hour he rode in the city, stopping randomly to enter and exit stores, changing cabs four times. Finally, convinced that he was not being followed, he purchased a newspaper and checked the classified ads over a beer in a neighborhood tavern.

Mitchell circled four small advertisements under the classification "Used Automobiles for Sale". It was after three by now but before four o'clock, he had purchased an eight-year old Volkswagen from a Munich plumber. Mitchell paid cash, and the title was signed over by the owner with none of the excessive written records that a new car purchase would have entailed. After a brief stop to pick up a few items of clothing and toiletries, Mitchell found himself on the Autobahn, moving steadily away from Munich to the Southeast. It was a route he had traveled before. He needed some time to sort out his thoughts . . . a place where he could relax for a few days.

At shortly after six-thirty, Mitchell drove into the town of Berchtesgaden.

Chapter 18.

To him, it had been the most beautiful place in the world. Now that he was about to see it again, he wondered if his positive recollections might have become exaggerated during the span of time since he'd last been there. Would the air really be as clean as he'd remembered, the mountains as tall, the meadows as green, the shops as quaint? He needed the reassurance of familiar settings.

It was a relief to him to recognize the church steeples of the small village nestled at the bottom of a valley surrounded on all sides by the alternately rocky and forested beauty of the Bavarian Alps. The familiarity of the street as he turned north along the Bahnhof Strabe was comforting. He wound his way through the business district in only a few minutes and turned on to the Salzburger Strabe. From among the numerous hotels and guest houses, he selected a small, quiet, unimposing but well-kept establishment. He pulled the Volkswagen into the lot behind the building.

The Haus Kurz had only ten rooms and seemed to Mitchell to be a perfect place to spend several days sorting out his thoughts without worry of outside interference. The interior of the building was modestly but cheerfully furnished and matched well the character of its stout, middle-aged owner.

She was sitting before the fireplace in the lobby as Mitchell came in, staring pensively at the crackling logs and dancing flame. The sight and smell of the burning pine filled the room and Mitchell was content to stand there quietly for a moment and absorb it.

The woman caught sight of him suddenly from the corner of her eye and rushed apologetically to the desk near the door.

"Oh, I'm so sorry," she said. "I hadn't heard you come in." She extended her hand. "My name is Anna Kurz."

"Franz Brandner," said Mitchell. "I'd like a room for a few days, if you have one."

"We have several." She gestured about the empty lobby. "Most of our guests left after . . . last night."

Mitchell felt as if she expected an explanation from him as to why he wasn't at home in mourning.

"I can understand that," he said. "As for me, I just couldn't get myself to face my normal schedule without a few days away from everything. I thought this might be a good spot for some quiet reflection."

Anna Kurz seemed to agree with that. "And where are you from Mr. Brandner?"

"Stuttgart."

She handed Mitchell the register and he signed it.

"I'll show you to your room."

"Please don't bother. I can find it."

"It's no trouble."

"You looked so comfortable when I came in . . . please sit down . . . I can find my way."

She reluctantly gave in. "Number six, second floor, on your right."

Mitchell walked up the staircase.

"You're welcome to use the lobby," she called. "We have a TV."

"Thank-you," Mitchell said.

He lay on the bed in his room for an hour staring at the ceiling and weighing the options open to him. Essentially, there were four possibilities.

He could give himself up.

He could wait an appropriate time and escape the country, living elsewhere under an assumed name.

He could contact a responsible party in the U.S. government and explain to them what had happened.

Mitchell didn't like any of the first three. The first and third would mean prison at the very least . . . the other, a life of constant running and hiding and looking over his shoulder.

He had still another choice. . . . Walker had given him the telephone number when they'd left Colorado. "Don't call unless you're instructed," he'd said. Mitchell opened his wallet. The numbers were listed in an address book, a different digit coded on separate pages. He could still try the number. What did he have to lose? He would be risking the possibility that, under the circumstances, international calls might be monitored by the German government. There was also the chance that the group who had set him up would trace the call to find his location. But despite those risks, the call offered Mitchell a hope . . . hope that an explanation could be made to clarify what had happened.

He got off the bed and locked the door behind him. He'd make the call.

Mitchell got change at a tavern, and headed north from Berchtesgaden. An hour later he pulled into a small town and stopped at a telephone booth near a quiet restaurant on the edge of town.

The pounding of his heart accelerated as he shut the

car door and walked the several yards to the phone booth. Beneath his feet, the sound of crunching gravel filled the chill night air. The door of the booth opened with a reluctant squawk. Mitchell deposited a coin and listened as the phone rang . . . twice . . . three times. . . .

"Operator."

"I'd like to make an international long distance call, please." His voice wavered to the extent it sounded as if it weren't coming from him. He breathed deeply several times in an effort to control it.

"Destination please,"

"The United States."

"I'll connect you with an overseas operator." There was a series of clicks as various connections were made and then the sound of ringing through the receiver.

"Overseas," the second operator answered.

"Go ahead, sir," the first said.

The thought occurred to Mitchell that operators world-wide sounded the same.

"I'd like to call the United States," he said. He gave the area code and number to the operator.

"Will you be paying for the call?"

"Yes."

"One moment."

Mitchell could hear the crisp snap of turning pages through the earpiece.

"May I have your number please?"

Mitchell hesitated. The number was printed plainly across the center of the dial. He became aware of the perspiration that was moist under his arms and had begun to trickle down his sides. He didn't want to give out the number. If it *were* to be traced, he wanted someone to have to work for it. Still, he had no choice. He gave her the number.

There was a silence at the other end, then the flipping

of more pages. "Twelve marks for three minutes," she said.

Mitchell put the coins into the phone, the chime registering each coin as it dropped.

"Thank you," the operator said as the last coin fell.

There was another, longer, series of clicks, then once again, the intermittent buzz and silence through the receiver that designated the ring at the other end.

Yet another operator answered. "U.S. Overseas."

Mitchell's operator repeated the information and in a matter of seconds the number was being dialed.

A car turned on an adjacent corner, throwing its headlights suddenly upon the phone booth and then beyond it. Mitchell glanced at his watch. He'd been on the phone for over two and a half minutes. He was uncomfortable.

The phone continued to ring for what seemed to Mitchell an eternity. On the sixth ring, an audible click was heard and Mitchell stopped breathing for an instant as a voice at the other end began speaking.

Mitchell's anxiety turned to helpless desperation as an all-too-familiar voice intoned, "I'm sorry, but the number you have reached is not in service at this time. . . ."

The operator disconnected the line. "I'll try again," she said.

The recorded response was the same.

"Are you certain of your number, sir?" she asked.

"I'm certain," Mitchell said. "Can you please ask for local assistance?"

"One moment."

He'd been on the phone almost four minutes by the time a local Washington operator had tried the number twice more with identical results.

"I'm sorry sir," she said.

"Can you please tell me, Operator," Mitchell said, "why that number is no longer in service? Perhaps its been changed to another number?"

"One moment."

It was nearly two minutes later when the operator returned. "Sir?"

"Yes."

"This is rather odd . . . the number wasn't disconnected . . . there is no reference number . . . we simply have no such number listed . . . the number has never been assigned."

Mitchell was silent.

"You must have been given an incorrect number, sir. Perhaps you can double-check and get the correct number."

"Yes," said Mitchell. "I guess I've been given an incorrect number."

"I'm sorry sir."

Mitchell placed the receiver back gently onto its cradle. He stood there a moment, his head resting against the cool moistness of the glass booth.

The change dropping to the coin return roused him. He looked again at his watch. Six and a half minutes. He swept the coins from the return, then hurried to the car.

The temptation to ram the accelerator to the floor was nearly overpowering, but Mitchell forced himself to obey the speed limit on the return trip to Berchtesgaden.

At the same time Mitchell was being frustrated by an unanswered phone, Gustav Junger was speaking long distance from Munich.

"I lost him," he said.

Walker, on the other end of the line, registered no emotion. "How?"

"Lost in a crowd at the airport."

"Did he get on a plane?"

"I don't think so."

"You'll have to find him very quickly."

"Any suggestions?"

"Let's see if I have something that might give us a lead." Junger could hear Walker on the other end of the line flipping through sheets of paper. He waited for a response.

"Now here's a possibility. . . ." Walker said.

It was shortly after midnight when Mitchell stopped in front of a tavern near the guest house where he had registered earlier in the evening.

Mitchell was depressed again. He had allowed himself some optimism earlier, but realized now it had been foolish to do so. There was no such number. It had been a mistake to try the call.

The lobby was deserted when Mitchell finally let himself in. One dim light burned behind the desk and another in the second floor hallway above. Across the room, a few dying embers of the fireplace glowed through an ashen cover.

Mitchell crossed to the TV, turned it on, and sat in an easy chair with his feet propped on an ottoman. The TV came on too loudly and Mitchell cursed and reluctantly stumbled over to turn it down.

His chair sat beside the fireplace and even though it had long since ceased burning, the area was pleasantly warm and comfortable from the earlier fire.

The TV was featuring a replay of everything Mitchell had seen the preceding night. The telecast originated in Munich, and was coincidentally, the same channel Mitchell had watched at the Bayerischer Hof. The seemingly perpetual rerun stopped finally at three-thirty with the commentator's announcement that a fifteen minute news summary would precede signoff.

Mitchell had been dozing but he rallied for the news.

The blue Volkswagen had been discovered in Schwabing that afternoon, the announcer said. While it contained the equipment used in the assassination, authorities had not been able to trace it any further than identifying it as a car which had been stolen two days earlier in Augsburg.

The announcer continued. "Germany's new Chancellor, Frederich Schelling, made his first public statement this afternoon to a grieving country."

The picture dissolved from the commentator to the office of the Chancellor. Frederich Schelling was a picture of dignity at his newly acquired desk. As he spoke, the camera moved closer, gradually revealing a lean, studious-looking man in his mid-fifties. His voice, though appropriately solemn, remained firm and resonant.

He explained that the next week would be one of national mourning for Karl Stehlin. He charged the German people to carry on with the same dedication and determination that had characterized Karl Stehlin.

Impressive man, thought Mitchell. Very eloquent.

All the while Schelling spoke, the camera moved steadily closer, until now, the torso of the man filled the screen.

Mitchell shifted uncomfortably in his seat.

Schelling pledged his firm conviction to devote his time and talent for the good of Germany.

Still the camera closed in.

Mitchell straightened up, sitting on the edge of his chair. He shook the grogginess from his head and squinted to clear the distortion of drunkenness from his vision. He had seen that man before! Why it should bother him, he didn't know. Schelling was obviously a prominent German politician. He might have seen his picture on any of a dozen different occasions. Still. . .

Schelling vowed sincerely that his government, with the help of God and the cooperation of the German people, would solve the problems confronting Germany and would lead the country into its greatest period of prosperity and world leadership.

The camera moved ever closer. The head of Frederich Schelling now filled the screen.

Suddenly Mitchell's mouth fell open. He formed a circle with the first finger and thumb of his left hand and raised it slowly to his right eye until the circle enclosed the face on the screen.

Mitchell dropped his hand and closed his eyes. The face within the boundaries of his circled fingers flashed into his mind. Only gradually, as he visualized it now, did the inner circumference of the circle through which he viewed the face, change from flesh to metal. And only subtly did the background behind the face change from a quiet office to that of a busy restaurant.

Mitchell slumped forward with his head in his hands. He could see it quite clearly now . . . could see the face which the scope had passed over fleetingly last night before stopping on Karl Stehlin. There was no mistaking it. It had been the face of Frederich Schelling.

Mitchell sagged back into the chair. The announcer went on to the local news wrap-up.

The implications of Schelling's presence at Irmgard's last night was as ominous as it was obvious. The man at the table almost *had* to know what was going to happen. That was the only way anyone could be certain that Karl Stehlin would be the man on the left.

Another point came to mind so forcefully now that Mitchell didn't see how he'd failed to note the omission when he read the early accounts of the assassination.

There had been *no* reference to who had been dining with the Chancellor when he died.

Mitchell now understood why.

His mind spinning from that realization, Mitchell was hardly prepared for the next local news item.

A spectacular accident near downtown Munich claimed the life of a young Stuttgart businessman early this morning. Erich Werner, thirty-five, apparently lost control of his auto while heading east over Maximiliansbrucke and plunged through the guard rail into the Isar River.

Officials estimated the Werner auto had probably gone into the river forty-five minutes before the accident was discovered. Due to the lack of traffic at that late hour, it was not discovered until 3:00 a.m. when a routine police patrol noted the damaged guard rail.

Death was attributed to injuries incurred in the crash.

Suddenly, at three-forty-five in the morning, David Mitchell was remarkably sober.

Chapter 19.

At exactly ten o'clock the next morning the Berchtesgaden Public Library opened its doors. Slightly more than thirty-six hours had passed since the assassination.

Dave Mitchell had been on the steps outside the library since nine o'clock. The librarian, a thin, sallow man of fifty, let himself in at nine-thirty. Mitchell had watched through the glass door as the librarian filed books and sorted cards and otherwise made certain he kept busy, lest the anxious man looking in from the outside try to catch his attention and ask to be admitted before the official opening time.

It had not been a restful night for Mitchell and it showed. His haste to get to the library as early as possible had brought him to the front door hung over, unshaven and generally unkempt. The librarian's condescending manner as he opened the door couldn't be misinterpreted.

The door had not yet closed behind them when Mitchell asked, "Do you carry subscriptions for the *Frankfurter Allgemeine, Suddeutsche Zeitung, Frankfurter Rundschau* and *Die Welt*?"

The papers he mentioned were the most highly regarded national papers in Germany and the librarian was taken a bit by surprise that such a disheveled individual as this would be aware of the existence of them, much less ever read them.

"We have them with the exception of the *Rundshau*," the librarian answered politely.

"Can I see copies of the past two day's issues for each of them and any other national papers you have?"

"We also subscribe to *Bild Zeitung*."

Mitchell nodded. "That too. Do you have this morning's issues yet?"

"The Hamburg papers won't be in until this afternoon."

"I'd appreciate it if you'd bring me whatever you can."

In a few moments the librarian had brought Mitchell copies of yesterday's issue for all four papers and the current morning issues of the two that were available. Mitchell stacked the papers in sequence and began to work his way deliberately through them.

He finished the first paper and laid it aside, going carefully, precisely through the next.

It was in the fourth paper that he found what he was looking for. It was a relatively extensive article, occupying eight paragraphs and was one of a dozen articles in that issue of *Die Welt* dealing with a variety of aspects concerning the assassination. The headline grabbed Mitchell's eye the moment he opened the page.

CONSPIRACY?

The widow of a prominent Hamburg attorney revealed today that her husband, the late Alwin Reichert received information last year from an unknown source concerning a conspiracy against the German government.

Speaking on a Hamburg radio station, Frau Maria Reichert stated that her husband had spent over two hours in discussion one evening last December with a stranger who called at their Hamburg residence.

According to Frau Reichert, her husband later revealed the gentleman in question had called to stress his concern of a planned conspiracy to topple the German government. The goal of the conspirators was reportedly to shift control within the German government and ultimately, with cooperation from unspecified outside sources, to effect the balance of power throughout Europe.

Frau Reichert said her husband was skeptical, but suggested the source report his information to police and the media. This advice apparently was not heeded.

In February, according to Frau Reichert, her husband mentioned that the man in question had died in an automobile accident. Several weeks later Herr Reichert himself died of a heart attack.

"I only felt that under the circumstances, I should make this bit of information public," said Frau Reichert.

Police and government agencies investigating the assassination of Karl Stehlin have subsequently commented that they have no indications of conspiracy to substantiate Frau Reichert's story.

A spokesman for one government investigating agency stated, "It's our job to keep records on possible subversive groups. Very little happens that we aren't aware of. It's nearly impossible that any serious conspiracy could exist without our knowledge of it."

Mitchell read it again, set the paper aside and went on

to the final two copies he had before him. When he finished going through them all, he stacked the papers and after reading the article in *Die Welt* a final time, placed it on top and returned the stack to the librarian.

The tone of the newspaper articles pointed out several things. Pressure on the investigative agencies to produce results were mounting. That pressure was being keenly felt at all levels. It was an ironic situation. All the evidence had been left behind. It had been turned inside out. It had been dusted and photographed and traced and measured and weighed and X-rayed and examined by the best in the business. Unfortunately, everything they had provided no leads as to who might have done it—or why.

The weapon in question had been traced to a U.S. Army unit in France, where it had been reported as stolen, along with thirteen other rifles and several thousand rounds of ammunition some five months previously. Neither French police nor military investigators had been able to produce any leads on the theft.

The scope and silencer on the weapon had been custom made and could have been produced in any country in the world.

The glass cutter, rope, gloves and key were all common German-made items that could have been purchased at any of a thousand shops throughout the country. A request for information from anyone having sold such items in the past few months had produced one report from a Bavarian mountaineer club that had lost several quality ropes in a break-in at one of their equipment stations high in the Austrian Alps.

Officers theorized that two other items, namely the glass cutter and gloves, were most likely stolen to prevent the possibility of anyone recalling a person to whom they'd sold such merchandise.

The keys could have been made anywhere.

And as previously reported, the blue Volkswagen had been stolen three days earlier in Augsburg. No witnesses.

No witnesses—that was the key. No one had recalled anyone buying the rope or glass cutter or gloves or keys. No one had seen anyone stealing the car. No one had seen anyone running from Peterskirche. No one had seen anyone leaving the VW in Schwabing. No witnesses!

So the German investigators sat helplessly, surrounded by everything associated with the crime except the person or persons responsible and the motive for doing it.

Generally, the investigators agreed, despite the apparently flawless execution of the plan, it was probably done by one deranged person acting on his own. Perhaps a person of Nazi persuasion or some similarly fanatical fringe group. The killer probably had military training and though presumably unbalanced, was nonetheless a cunning and calculating planner as well as an expert rifle shot.

The theories of conspiracy from within Germany were agreed to be without foundation.

The theory of assassination by elements of a foreign government, if it had come to mind at all, was dismissed as groundless and not mentioned as a legitimate possibility.

And there was still no mention from any source as to who had been dining with the Chancellor on that fatal night.

The glass door of the library closed behind Mitchell and he welcomed the fresh breeze that hit his face. He made his way down the curving sidewalk that wound to the main business district.

Mitchell crossed to a small park and sat on the ground at the base of a gigantic tree and lit a cigarette.

He laid his head back against the gnarled trunk and exhaled. The smoke from his nostrils disintegrated in the clean mountain air. Mitchell sat engrossed in thought.

The account in *Die Welt* of the possible conspiracy had been the type of article Mitchell had been seeking when he went to the library. The uncertainty of the past few days seemed to be settling now. The conclusion Mitchell was beginning to accept wasn't necessarily a comforting one. Nevertheless, it appeared to be the solution to a puzzle that couldn't be adequately explained otherwise.

Mitchell shook his head in bitter wonder. The similarities in Frau Reichert's newspaper account and Walker's explanation to Mitchell were remarkably alike, too much alike to be coincidental. Based on the evidence as he saw it now, the newspaper account was probably true. And accepting that as fact, it followed that Walker's explanation relating to the existence of the group was true as well.

Mitchell closed his eyes and massaged the bridge of his nose with his left hand. He exhaled loudly and stretched his legs as he sat. The fatigue he'd been fighting for the past two days was beginning to show now. Added to that, his realization of what had really happened brought a great weariness over him. For a few moments he felt as if he didn't care what might happen next.

He shook it off and got up and began walking through the park in an effort to clear his head.

How did it all shake down then?

First, he thought there *was* a conspiracy. The organization planning the takeover of the government did exist. The fact Mitchell had been recruited to assassinate the Chancellor was definitive proof of that. It also seemed obvious now that Walker was a member of the group. Mitchell had been set up to commit what was probably the first major step in the group's move to assume control. The man who was now the German Chancellor was also a member of the group and was the one who had enabled the set-up of Karl Stehlin to tke place.

So what happens next?

Two things. The organization must get rid of the only man outside the organization who knows what happened—namely, David Mitchell—and the organization must put their succeeding plans into motion.

Mitchell stood in the quiet of the park for a moment staring up at the giant snow-covered crags that encircled Berchtesgaden.

Chapter 20.

Mitchell had reached a decison on what he must do next. He sifted the specifics through his mind as he watched the sporadic traffic that moved along the street that fronted the park. Suddenly, his train of thought was shattered.

A block away, a green Porsche moved very deliberately down the street.

Mitchell shifted his position uneasily. It's impossible, he thought. A coincidence.

But the closer the Porsche came to the middle of the block, the more certain Mitchell was that it was the same car that followed him in Munich. Mitchell walked casually to the base of a large elm tree that blocked the view from the street.

The Porsche passed by. A man in a white sweater looked out the windows from side to side.

Mitchell slipped away from the elm when the car had gone by. He started at a brisk walking pace, then ran to the parking lot.

In the rear view mirror of the Porsche, Gustav Junger's peripheral vision picked up a blur of movement behind him. He slowed the car and turned to look over his left shoulder. It looked as though a man had run behind a stand of trees near the center of the park. Junger pulled the car over to the curb and got out, closing the door quietly behind him.

He was halfway to the trees when he saw an old Volkswagen pulling out of a lot behind the park—a lot he hadn't seen from the other street. The car was nearly a hundred yards away from him. Junger had no idea who was in it. He knew of only one way to find out. He charged straight at the car. If it were a tourist or a citizen of Berchtesgaden, they probably wouldn't notice him at this distance. But if it was Werner. . .

Mitchell had disappeared by the time Junger got to the Porsche. But Junger had found what he wanted to know. Mitchell was in Berchtesgaden, and was driving a tan Volkswagen, four or five years old.

Junger threw the car in gear and circled the park to the lot. He sped to his right, down the street into which Mitchell had turned. It wound for several blocks and then forked into two directions. One turned and headed back to the center of town. The other ribboned its way up into the mountains. Junger hesitated a moment. A man in flight usually left the place in which he'd been discovered. It was strictly a guess. He took the mountain path.

Further up the road, the Volkswagen labored along the steep incline. Cursing, Mitchell let up on the gas pedal and then pushed it down again. The car sputtered, then caught itself and surged forward. In a few hundred yards it lost power and Mitchell repeated the process. Above him, the road hairpinned back and forth up the side of the mountain.

Mitchell pulled to the shoulder of the road and looked over the edge at the twisting ribbon of highway below him.

It took a moment to spot it—a moment in which

Mitchell allowed himself to think that his pursuer had taken the wrong turn. But there, less than a mile and a half behind him, the Porsche climbed effortlessly up the hill. Mitchell looked above him. He was no more than two-thirds of the distance to the summit.

Gustav Junger, an experienced mountain driver, took the turns at high speed with the ease of someone out for a Sunday drive.

Mitchell thought for a moment, then pulled the car back on the road, turned around, and headed downhill.

It nearly worked. So intent had been Gustav Junger on the road ahead of him that he had passed the tan Volkswagen before it registered on him that it was the same vehicle he was pursuing. He slammed on the brakes and spun the Porsche around in the middle of the road.

Mitchell put the accelerator of the Volkswagen to the floor, but the downhill speed was more than he could handle. He backed off the accelerator. In the rear view mirror, he could see the Porsche steadily gaining ground. It was less than a quarter of a mile behind him.

There was no way he could outdistance it. He might kill himself if he tried.

A dirt side road came up suddenly on his left. Mitchell hit the brakes and veered sharply off the main road. The dust rose up in a thick curtain as the wheels spun gravel and Mitchell disappeared into the trees.

There was a possibility that Junger would miss the turn. But through the mirror, Mitchell saw another cloud of dust rise up two hundred yards behind him. Junger had seen the dust kicked up when Mitchell turned off the road. It was only a matter of moments before he would overtake Mitchell.

In a last ditch effort to lose his pursuer, Mitchell pulled the car off the dirt roadway. The Volkswagen whined as it labored over the rough terrain, scraping branches and tree trunks as it bounced into the thick forest.

Gustav Junger caught a glimpse of the Volkswagen through an opening in the trees some one hundred yards ahead. Without hesitation, he veered off the road and headed into the forest after Mitchell. The rock strewn surface jarred and tossed the Porsche, but Junger barged on.

The terrain was quickly becoming impassable. Large rocks loomed up and with tangled fallen trees, blocked any further access to the south. On Mitchell's immediate right, a cliff rose up sharply. Behind him, and to his left, the Porsche banged relentlessly forward.

Mitchell jerked the car to a halt, got out, and ran. He ran straight ahead into the forest, leaping over fallen trees and dodging around boulders. He ran steadily, confidently. He was no match for the man behind him in a car. But on the ground, running across the uneven mountain terrain, Mitchell felt as if he were back on the obstacle course in Colorado. He ran at nearly full speed down a sloping ridge, then veered to his right up a small ravine.

Gustav Junger was out of the Porsche and running a half minute behind Mitchell. The change from automobile to foot didn't faze him. It was a routine part of the job. As he pounded along Mitchell's trail, he wished that his shoes provided greater traction. He filed it away as something to act on later.

Mitchell ran without effort up the ravine. But as he moved further into it, the sides suddenly became quite steep. He wondered if he had made a mistake in entering the ravine. He looked behind him while he ran.

In the distance he caught glimpses of the man in the white sweater.

Junger pulled the pistol from inside his jacket. He could probably get a shot at him if the ravine straightened out for any length. He considered it as he ran. But that would make more trouble for him than he wanted. His orders were to take Werner alive. He slipped the pistol back into the holster and picked up the pace. He exhaled loudly a few times. Werner was in better shape than Junger had expected.

Mitchell, still running easily, bolted around a turn on the hard sandstone bottom of the ravine. Fifty yards ahead of him, the ravine ended. He surveyed it as he ran. One side had crumbled slightly. A small shrub grew out of the bank some five feet up. It was nearly an equal distance from the shrub to the top of the ravine.

Mitchell went into it at full speed, springing off the mounded earth that had collapsed from the side as if it were a ramp. He soared into the air, his opposite foot catching the shrub that protruded from the bank. He pushed off it hard, in one continuing motion. He felt the shrub snap beneath him, but its support had been firm enough to enable him to get the upper half of his body over the ravine wall. Kicking and scrambling, he pulled himself over the top and rolled away from the edge.

Junger rounded the turn as Mitchell disappeared over the top.

"Werner!" he called. "Don't run! I'm here to help you! I'm your contact!"

Mitchell moved further away from the edge of the ravine and got to his feet. The words of the man behind him did not comfort Mitchell. He knew his contact was dead. He looked around for his next move.

On both sides, the mountains rose up in abrupt, vertical cliffs. Ahead of him, only thirty or forty yards, the ground fell away just as precipitously. He peered over the edge to a valley floor at least a hundred feet below. The alternatives were limited. He looked to his right at a six inch ledge that ran for ten yards along the edge of the cliff that soared above the valley. Beyond the ledge were several rocky protrusions, spaced for approximately another ten yards. At that point there was a cut back into the cliff. From where Mitchell stood it looked as though it widened into another ravine similar to the one he had just come through. As he viewed it, it was his only option. Without looking down, he stepped out onto the ledge. It was only wide enough for a toe hold. Mitchell turned slightly sideways and stepped out with his lead foot, then slid the other up to it. He pressed his body against the rock and carefully began to make his way across the chasm.

Behind him, Gustav Junger was clawing himself out of the ravine. Mitchell worked tenuously along the precipice. Pebbles loosened beneath his feet and dropped into the valley below. He pressed closer to the cliff wall. The muscles in his arms and legs knotted under the strain.

The ledge ended, and Mitchell groped for toe-holds. His hands were scraped and sore as he dug his fingers into any small opening in the rock. His fear of falling was exceeded only by his fear of the man behind him. Mitchell forced himself to take the first step off the ledge. He clung to the wall like a spider, groping his way toward the opening in the cliff that was now so close, yet so far away.

As Mitchell was reaching for the last hand hold, a puffing, red-faced Gustav Junger looked out over the edge of the cliff.

With a lunge, Mitchell reached the rocky opening and pulled himself to safety, out of view from the other side. Bruised and bleeding, he took off up the ravine.

Gustav Junger challenged the cliff as he challenged everything—head-on.

He had gone nearly a third of the way before he

learned something about himself that he had never known before.

He was afraid of heights.

It was more than simply a healthy respect for them. Gustav Junger was nearly immobilized by fear.

Only his iron will enabled him to pull himself together.

He called on all his resources and moved his foot ever-so-slightly forward. He took another step . . . a little further this time.

When he reached safety, he fell on the ground and crawled well away from the edge of the cliff. He sat for a moment, pulling himself together. The chase had taken its toll on Junger. The incident at the ledge had further sapped his strength.

Far ahead of him, Mitchell had caught his second wind and raced like a deer out of the ravine and back into the forest. He felt a sense of exhilaration and power in knowing he had won.

Junger knew it as well. He began running up the ravine but in only a few minutes he slowed to a trot . . . then a walk.

When he finally returned to where they had left the cars, the Volkswagen was gone. The tires on the Porsche were flat. The distributor had been yanked out. The carburetor was smashed.

Junger, with his feet back on the ground, had regained his bearings. He admired Werner's thoroughness. Junger himself should have thought to incapacitate the Volkswagen when he had first gotten out to give chase on foot.

He had underestimated this man. It was the second time he had gotten away from him.

Junger began walking back toward the highway. He stopped by a stream and splashed cold mountain water on his face. Refreshed, he continued on. He would have to make a phone call when he got to Berchtesgaden. He didn't look forward to that. He shrugged. No one had said it would be an easy job.

Chapter 21.

Mitchell was well into the Bavarian Alps, heading northwest of Berchtesgaden. He had stopped in a small town an hour earlier and traded his Volkswagen to a used car dealer for a newer model of a different color. It ran smoothly along the autoban.

A roadsign ahead gave distances to several cities. His eyes focused on one:

Bonn—380 Km.

He glanced at his watch. He would be there by early evening if he drove steadily.

As the hours and miles slipped by him, he revised and polished his plan. He knew that any ideas he came up with before he actually had a chance to look at things firsthand might have to be changed once he arrived. How it's done isn't really so important anyway, thought Mitchell. There'll be ways to do it, and when I get there, I'll pick the best one.

From travel brochures Mitchell picked up in Heidelberg, he decided to stop first in Bad Godesberg in south suburban Bonn. Bad Godesberg, located conveniently near the Gouvernmental Quarter, served as home for numerous foreign residences and missions as well as providing a meeting ground for students, artists and miscellaneous wanderers.

Mitchell, fitting into the last two categories, rented a small apartment in a modest, unobtrusive area of town, again using the name of Franz Brandner and paying a month's rent in advance to set the landlord's mind at ease.

Unfortunately, the excellent identification he carried for Eric Werner was too risky to use now and it left Mitchell with nothing but the title of the car on which he'd used the Brandner name. He destroyed the Werner identification that night and the next morning set out to pick up some other items which he could use to substantiate his new identity.

A library card was no problem.

Immediately upon paying five hundred marks, Franz Brandner was welcomed as a member in good standing of the Drachenfels Sports Club, complete wih full restaurant, gymnasium, swimming, tennis and firing range privileges, and a membership card as well.

A new wallet, with his name embossed in gold across the inner fold, and the I.D. card that accompanied it, gave him enough documentation to obtain a driver's license that completed his list. It was clearly not as professional or as complete an identification as he'd had for Werner, but under the circumstances he would have to make do with it.

He browsed throughout the city for several more hours, stopping once at a drug store to purchase two hair dyes, one in dark brown, the other in his natural color.

He spent time looking through the sporting goods departments of several downtown stores and later moved to outlying areas. And while the clerks brought out an endless parade of the latest equipment and clothing, Mitchell studied the gun racks and mentally stored the floor plans and any security devices he could make out. When he could, he accompanied the clerks on their searches for equipment into rear storerooms, where he noted as much as possible about alarm systems, and occasionally, the lack of them.

By day's end, Mitchell had acquired enough information on the ski industry to go into business for himself. Of greater importance, he knew of at least a dozen shops that stocked high-powered hunting rifles. Three of them apparently had no electronic alarm system. He scribbled their addresses on the inside cover of a matchbook.

Mitchell began the drive back to Bad Godesberg at six o'clock. He took one short detour, turning onto Adenauerallee for his first look at the Gouvernmental Quarter. Situated between the broad thoroughfare on the west and the Rhine River on the east, the area was one of beautifully green and manicured grounds surrounding a blend of both classic and contemporary architecture.

In the midst of this sprawling layout was the Bundeskanzlerplatz. Directly north of it was the stately Palais Schaumburg, and at a further distance to the east, the Bundeshaus. The Chancellery and the house of the Federal President, Villa Hammerschmidt, were among the other buildings in the Quarter. The beautiful grounds, together with the variety of architectural design against the backdrop of the Rhine were compelling subjects to artists, or for that matter, to anyone who fancied himself to be one. Even at this hour of dusk, Mitchell noted the Bundeskanzlerplatz, with its central location and vantage point for several of the area's most interesting scenes, was sprinkled with a handful of easels.

Mitchell turned through the square and past the Palace and then past the Parliament onto the street that parallelled the west bank of the Rhine. A barge and a sightseeing boat heading slowly downstream passed in the opposite direction and it was quite and peaceful along the river. Mitchell drove north along the Rhine's west bank, absorbing the sights and smells, past the Gouvernmental Quarter, all the way to the Kennedybrucke which spanned the river at Meckenheimer Strabe, then turned and drove once again southward down Adenauerallee, out of Bonn and back to Bad Godesberg.

Mitchell passed two weeks without leaving his small apartment. The mustache and beard he had been allowing to grow unchecked for the past sixteen days was filling in nicely. He had brought the brown hair coloring out of the medicine cabinet, dying his hair and tinting the facial stubble as well as he could, then trimming it back to a respectable neatness.

The following day, Mitchell ventured out to Rolandseck where he bought an easel, palate, sketch pads, pencils, brushes, paints, canvases and various other art supplies.

At three-thirty in the afternoon, equipment under his arm, he strolled into the Bundeskanzlerplatz and set up his gear across from the Palais Schaumburg. He was pleased to see that the activity he'd noticed on the first day he viewed the Quarter was apparently typical. Scattered throughout the square were at least a half-dozen other artists or students sketching and painting with an informality that marked them as an integral part of the daily routine of the Quarter.

Mitchell had taken some art courses in college and had in fact done some free lance art which eventually led to his career in the agency business. With that background, distant though it was, he felt he could fit into the Bundeskanzlerplatz without attracting undue attention.

And so, each day at varying times, Mitchell arrived in

the Bundeskanzlerplatz where he sat working casually but steadily at a variety of scenes, alternately sketching and painting in oil or water colors until darkness descended upon the square. In a small notebook he kept in his trouser pocket, he made notes about the activities that occurred throughout the Quarter, particularly those revolving around the Chancellery and the Bundeshaus. He felt quite inconspicuous in his role in the square. An artist gazing thoughtfully about the Bundeskanzlerplatz was not an unusual occurrence and no one seemed to pay any more heed to him than to the other fixed surroundings in the square.

At the same time, he wondered how long it would be before his pursuers relocated him.

But he couldn't allow himself to dwell on that. He had a job to do. It was only a matter of time till he'd learn what he needed to know.

Chapter 22.

The clerk at the Bayerischer Hof was a little unnerved by the steely stare of the man in front of the desk. He flipped through the reservation book a second time even though he knew the information the tall man had requested was not there. He looked up and shook his head apologetically.

"I'm sorry sir," he said. "Mr. Werner checked out last week, but he left no forwarding address."

Walker's expression didn't change. He spoke quietly, as if he didn't want to trouble anyone. Yet something in his tone reflected an authority that demanded action. "Is there somewhere else that you might record a forwarding address?"

"I'll check one other possibility, sir." The clerk disappeared into a room behind the desk. He waited there a moment and then returned. "I'm sorry," he said. "We have no forwarding address."

Walker hadn't expected any. It was a long shot that had to be checked out.

"Thank you for your trouble," he said. He turned and walked out of the hotel.

The clerk noted how perfect his posture was.

Outside, Frank Walker took a seat on a bench along the Promenadeplatz and considered his next move.

Chapter 23.

Gustav Junger was never late for an appointment. Neither was the man he was meeting.

Junger looked at his watch and hurried along the street to insure that he would be on time.

Both men had taken extreme precaution in arriving at the meeting site. They had doubled back, gone through crowded stores, changed cabs and doubled back again. This relatively complicated process was strictly routine to them.

They arrived at "Heinrich's," an out of the way cafe just outside Munich, at almost the same time, each within a minute of seven o'clock. From halfway down the block, Junger saw the door close behind his boss.

He stepped up the pace, glancing habitually over his shoulder as he stepped through the door.

There were only a few scattered guests seated in the dining room. Junger spotted his man at the far corner table. The waiter took him over.

Walker stood and extended his hand. "Good to see you," he said.

"Same here," Junger replied. "You look well."

"I try to keep fit," Walker said.

They sat down and Walker ordered a drink. Junger passed.

"What happened?" asked Walker. The preliminary amenities were apparently out of the way.

Junger told the story exactly as it had taken place.

When he finished, Walker sipped at his drink for several moments before he responded. "We have to find him soon."

"Can we call in some help?"

Walker shook his head. "Too sensitive. We can't let anyone else in on it. And we can't afford the risk of stirring up a lot of activity after something like this has happened." He shook his head again. "We have to find him ourselves."

"Where do we start?"

"I've got a lot of data on him. His whole life history. How he's reacted to various situations throughout his life. Personality and psychology tests. I'm having it run through the computer with every possible alternative I could think he might consider."

"How soon will we have that?"

"A few days," said Walker. "They have to program everything first. Then, based on what's happened, and what the computer knows about him, we get the most likely course of action that he'd take."

Junger wasn't completely comfortable with a machine making that kind of judgment.

"Its input comes from me," said Walker. "I spent a lot of time thinking about it."

"What do we do in the meantime?" asked Junger.

"Check out airports, bus stations, railroad terminals. Look around Munich. Check out the Werner apartment in Frankfort. Keep an eye on his girlfriend in Schwabing and the other places that were his favorite spots here."

"Where should I start?"

"Since you're up to date on where he went around here, you check out Munich. I'll go to Frankfort for a day or two. Let's meet back here at the same time on Wednesday night."

"Do you think he believes he was set up?" asked Junger.

"There's no doubt in his mind," said Walker.

They ordered dinner and ate in silence.

Three nights later at seven o'clock, the two men were once again seated at Heinrich's.

"Find anything?" asked Walker.

Junger replied negatively. "How about you?"

"Nothing from my trip. But I did hear from the computer."

Junger leaned forward. "Well?"

"We're going to Bonn."

"Why Bonn?"

"Because that's where the computer says he went. And it makes sense to me. I believe it."

"What's he doing in Bonn?" Junger asked.

Walker leaned over the table and spoke in a whisper. "He's there to assassinate the Chancellor of West Germany."

Chapter 24.

Mitchell wondered if he'd gone mad.

Just over a month ago his biggest problems had been determining creative approaches, budget allocations, and media mixes in the frozen food business. Though he'd never taken it too seriously, he had still held it to be a substantial responsibility.

Today, he was in the capital of West Germany to assassinate the man who had taken over the reins of government from the man he had assassinated two days ago.

The early days that followed the assassination had seemed like a bad dream from which Mitchell felt he'd certainly awaken. But the passing of time had forced the reality upon him. He recognized that time spent in wishing things had happened differently—or in hoping things would change—was time wasted.

The fact he'd been used . . . deceived . . . probably weighed on him harder than any other. He liked to think of himself as possessing a certain amount of sophistication to complement what he felt was his greatest asset —common sense. It was difficult to admit he was naive enough to be set up as he had been. The only consolation—and it was of very little comfort to him—was the face he'd been taken in by a first-rate organization.

To try and make up for the mistake seemed the only alternative. The possible consequences were grim but Mitchell preferred them to the options he had in other areas.

If he did nothing, the conspiracy would continue their plans. Whether they would move prudently over a matter of time, or quickly, to take advantage of the present unsettled atmosphere was a matter of speculation. Regardless, the end result would be the same. The goal of the conspiracy would finally be realized. Mitchell, meanwhile, would be a marked man to that group for the rest of his life.

If he went to the authorities to explain what had happened, he expected he'd live less than twenty-four hours. The organization would doubtlessly be involved as soon as any suspects were taken into custody. The risk of "accidents" occuring in that situation were limitless. The recently reported deaths of Gustav Junger and Eric Werner were proof of that. And if, by the remotest of chances, he were able to tell his story, he had no hard evidence to back it up. Even having lived through the experience, it was difficult for Mitchell to understand everything that happened. How then, could he expect others to believe it with only his word as proof?

If, on the other hand, he assassinated Frederich Schelling, the German government would certainly be in turmoil. But to an even greater degree, the conspiracy would be in turmoil. If what Walker had originally told Mitchell of the group was true, the death of the real "Big Red" would virtually eliminate the Conspiracy as a threat, leaving only leaderless, independent cells with no common bond. Based on the lack of information regarding a country-wide conspiracy, Mitchell tended to believe that each cell did exist independently and without knowledge of any other. Thus, eliminating Frederich Schelling would eliminate the threat.

Mitchell had analyzed the possibilities.

Suppose Walker's details regarding the conspiracy were all lies. The group might in reality be well organized and disciplined with a known chain of command that included the highest position in the German government.

But even if Walker had lied, the assassination of Frederich Schelling would throw a huge wrench into *any* conspiratorial plans, no matter how they were organized or formulated. The death of two German Chancellors within a month would bring the theory of conspiracy to the front of the world's headlines. Tremendous pressure would be brought about to identify and destroy the conspirators. An outraged and frightened public would demand it. A grim and concerned legislature would demand it. A thorough military and governmental investigation would uncover it. It was inevitable.

As far as the personal consequences for Mitchell, he would be sought regardless of what happened from this point on.

Chapter 25.

Two weeks in Bonn passed into a third. On a cloudy Wednesday afternoon that hinted of rain, Mitchell arrived in the square, riding for the first time on a small used motorcycle he'd purchased five days earlier. The full beard and mustache had flourished during past weeks and did a commendable job of hiding the recognizable features of David Mitchell.

He set up his equipment on the east side of the square as was his habit. An outward appearance of calm masked a growing feeling of anticipation. He looked over his shoulder with more regularity.

He put several completed drawings and paintings inside the pad beside him and began, almost automatically, what would be his sixth painting of the Palace. The advantage of repetition of subjects was showing up favorably in his work and his last dozen projects of various scenes throughout the Quarter were quite good. He had, in fact, sold a few of his recent works to passersby in the square.

He began this effort on the Palace with a bold, sure stroke.

A week ago, Mitchell had decided how he'd do it.

The notebook, after more than two weeks, was

jammed with times and dates of the Chancellor's coming and going. Taken as they occurred, they appeared too haphazard to predict. Even after setting the activities on a daily sheet, week by week, the lack of routine was remarkable. Probably by design, the new Chancellor kept a most erratic itinerary.

He arrived in the morning at any time from seven to ten o'clock. He left for lunch between eleven and two. Occasionally he didn't go out for lunch at all. In the evening, he left as early as four o'clock and as late as nine. On two days, he hadn't come in at all. It was obvious that the schedule was juggled for security reasons. And when Frederich Schelling did appear, it was never without an entourage of secret service agents.

There had been only one exception.

For the first two weeks, the Chancellor's limousine picked him up at seven-thirty on Wednesday evening and left the Quarter heading north on Wilhelm-Spiritus-Ufer.

On the second Wednesday, when the limousine pulled up in front of the Chancellery at seven-twenty-five, Mitchell had picked up his materials and when the huge black car pulled out at seven-thirty, Mitchell, on his motorcycle, followed at a distance of several blocks.

With the maneuverability of the motorcycle and the ease in spotting the limousine, Mitchell was able to follow at a distance great enough to insure he wouldn't be detected. The limousine crossed the Rhine on the Kennedybrucke, then turned back in a southward direction. In ten minutes, it had pulled up beneath a canopy in front of a distinguished old building on Limpericher Strabe. A doorman greeted the car and one of the two security men with the Chancellor, a security man who apparently doubled as driver on these Wednesday night sojourns, left the car and entered the building. As

Mitchell passed by, he noticed the Chancellor and the other security man remained in the back seat of the limousine.

Mitchell gave a fleeting glance at the building.

The metal plate at the side of the door read simply, "Schumann Club." He continued southward down the street.

The Schumann Club faced east. Across Limpericher Strabe, one of the many city parks that contributed to Bonn's reputation as the world's greenest capital, unfolded pleasantly over several acres of gently rolling land dotted heavily with assorted trees and bushes.

Mitchell turned on the street that bordered the southern edge of the park and then turned back to the north on the Neustrabe which was the easterly border of the park. Mitchell parked his motorcycle at an entrance on Neustrabe, where, although he couldn't see it through the foliage, he estimated he was almost directly on a line opposite the Schumann Club.

He made his way through the park as purposefully as possible without attracting attention and within a few minutes came round a clump of lilac bushes that set halfway up a small grass covered knoll amidst a scattered cluster of huge, straight pines. Less than a hundred yards directly to his front, was the main entrance to the Schumann Club. The limousine was just pulling out of the drive and into what appeared to be a rear parking lot. The Chancellor and the second security man had apparently gone into the building.

He spent another hour wandering through the park until dusk settled over the area. There were few persons in the park and those who were there seemed to gather mostly near a pond at the northern edge, several hundred yards from Mitchell's location. The view of the pond from where he stood was obscured by random groupings of pine.

The group had not yet left the Schumann Club. Mitchell fished a cigarette from a half empty pack and walked back to the bunch of lilacs across from the club. It was a thick stand, probably nine feet tall and covering a circular area of fifteen to twenty feet. Mitchell moved closer to the bushes and sat down on the grass beside them. This particular spot was removed from the several bicycle and walking paths that crossed the park. Rarely did anyone pass within close proximity to where he sat.

The patch of lilacs was indeed thick. Mitchell couldn't see through to the other side. The base of the bushes at ground level however, were each a few feet apart. Mitchell put his cigarette out on the ground and stuck the butt in his shirt pocket. He took a careful look about him in all directions and satisfying himself that no one was watching, Mitchell turned over onto his stomach and crawled through the small opening between the bases of the bushes. They were planted in a circular pattern, but in a random manner and Mitchell had to force his way inside. He inched along until he reached an area with enough head clearance to allow himself to sit upright comfortably. He was surrounded on all sides by thick foliage, but as he pushed a branch in front of him slightly to one side, the lighted canopy of the Schumann Club, centered in a frame of leaves and branches, came into view.

Mitchell exhaled silently and brought his arm back to his side. The branch returned to its normal position, blocking out the frontal view and enveloping him in darkness.

This was the place.

It was apparently the only place where the Chancellor made it a point to be at the same time each week. It was away from the Gouvernmental Quarter with its scores of security people. There was perfect cover for him to set up a good escape route. Mitchell registered approval as he went over the details in his head. He'd make a dry run the next week and if everything checked out, the week following that would be the real thing.

He remained there for several more minutes and when he was certain that no one was around, he dropped again to his stomach and squirmed back out onto the grass.

He took his time crossing back to where he'd left his motorcycle. First, he estimated the distance from the bush to the front door of the club at eighty yards. Behind the bush, the park stretched another three hundred yards to Neustraße where he'd left his motorcycle. Too far to go after he'd fired the shots, he decided. He didn't want to have to leave the park on the dead run.

By the time Mitchell reached his motorcycle he'd decided how he'd do it.

It was, he thought, a rather simple and relatively secure plan.

A clock in the square chimed five as Mitchell began to fill in the final details of the painting that had materialized in front of him. The square was a flurry of activity as it was every day at this time as the workers in the Quarter left another business day behind them.

Then as the clock passed six and closed on seven it became the most restful time of day in the Bundeskanzlerplatz and the time that Mitchell enjoyed the most.

He completed the water color of the Palace and laid it aside and was well into a sketch of the Bundeshaus. His thoughts were on the time now and he sketched absently between glances at his watch. He'd leave about seven and get to the park early today for the dry run.

So detached was he, he didn't hear the footsteps that crossed the square and stopped behind him. The voice, when it spoke, was unexpected and it slashed like a knife into Mitchell's concentration. His hand jerked involuntarily across the pad in front of him.

"Excuse me," the man said. Then, seeing that he'd caused Mitchell to ruin the sketch, "I'm sorry. I didn't mean to startle you."

To say that Mitchell was startled was an understatement. His mind had been wandering ahead to the Schumann Club and his hand had been moving mechanically across the sketch pad and the voice, so abrupt and so close at hand, stunned him. An instant flashed before Mitchell realized he'd only been caught with the thoughts in his mind, and not at the actual deed.

The man remained looking over Mitchell's shoulder. Mitchell didn't turn to acknowledge him. He had made it a point to avoid conversations since he'd been in Bonn and now, as the clock in the square signaled seven, it was certainly no time to begin.

"It's all right," Mitchell said. "I was about to quit for the day anyway."

"Well I certainly feel badly about this," the voice said. "I appreciate the effort that goes into art."

Mitchell began gathering his things together and hoped the man would leave. "I have a dozen more like it," Mitchell said.

The man moved from behind Mitchell to his side. "Yes, I know," he said. "I've noticed that you come here regularly."

Mitchell could partially observe him with his peripheral vision and he looked up from his equipment now to see a strapping middle-aged man with a barrel chest and broad shoulders measuring him with narrowed eyes that penetrated from under thick, bushy eyebrows. He was short, with a ruddy complexion.

"I'm with the government," the man said.

Mitchell felt his muscles tense as he worked the easel into its case.

"That's how I've happened to see you here before,"

the man explained. "I work here in the Quarter."

Mitchell continued gathering his equipment.

"I've especially admired your water colors," the stout man said. "The reason I stopped by this evening was to see if I might purchase some of them from you. . . ." Mitchell's silence seemed to make him uncomfortable. "I'm really sorry about your sketch."

Mitchell looked carefully into the eyes of the man at his side. The sincerity and concern mirrored on the coarse features were either genuine or a faultless act.

"Don't worry about it," Mitchell said. He zippered the easel case and laid it on its side.

"I work in the Bundeshaus. I'm a clerk there," the man said. "That's how I've happened to see you here in the square."

Mitchell felt relief at learning what line of government work the robust man was in. Still, time was moving swiftly and he had no desire to make conversation.

"As I said," the man offered again, "I'd like to buy some of your work . . . particularly water colors of the Palace and the Bundeshaus."

Mitchell didn't have the time or inclination to haggle, but the prospect of extra cash was something that appealed to him. The funds he'd received in Munich were steadily depleting with no prospects of being replenished. While he was still comfortably set at the moment, it might take considerable expense for him to make a clean break and relocate from Germany after this thing was over.

He opened his sketch pad and made a quick count of the assorted drawings and water colors. "Fifteen here altogether," said Mitchell. "I'll give you the whole thing for four hundred marks." He was sure he'd priced himself out of consideration.

The clerk took the pad in his hands and leafed critically through the pages.

Mitchell picked up his easel and stood waiting.

"I really don't need them all. . . ." the man began.

"I'd rather not sell just one or two of them," Mitchell said. "I think they go together nicely as a group."

"Well, I don't know. . . ." the clerk reconsidered. "Perhaps I can think it over and see you tomorrow."

"As a matter of fact, today is my last day here," Mitchell said. "I'm moving to another area for a month or so." As he said it, Mitchell realized it would in fact be a good idea not to return to the square, particularly if someone like this clerk from the Bundeshaus was so aware of his presence. He closed the sketch pad and fit it under his arm.

"I don't want to rush off, but I have an appointment at seven-thirty."

"Oh, certainly," the clerk said, still deliberating.

Mitchell started the bike and set it in gear.

"I'll take it!" the clerk said suddenly. He took out his wallet and counted off four hundred marks.

With some surprise, Mitchell handed over the pad and took the four hundred marks. He thanked the man and hurried off for the Schumann Club. The Bundeshaus clerk, smiling to himself, walked slowly back across the square, thumbing contentedly through his newly acquired collection.

So engrossed was he in studying his new possessions that he nearly bumped into a tall, well-built man with graying hair, who had just entered the square on foot.

"Excuse me," the clerk said.

Walker seemed predisposed. He didn't reply, but continued walking on through the square, apparently looking for someone.

At twenty minutes after seven, Dave Mitchell looked carefully around the park in all directions, and finding himself clear, twisted his way inside the bushes. He sat waiting quietly, surrounded by the sweet smell of lilacs that filled the air.

Mitchell raised his arm slightly and brushed back the branch that exposed the small opening through the maze to the front of the Schumann Club. The doorman greeted a guest who arrived by cab and Mitchell brought his hand back to his side. The branch sprung back into place, shutting off the view from the outside. It was nearly seven-thirty.

At exactly seven-forty-two the limousine pulled up in front of the club. Mitchell looked on intently as the first security man, doubling as driver, got out of the car and entered the club by himself, just as he'd done the previous week. He returned in a minute and opened the rear door for the other two occupants.

Frederich Schelling was the first one out, then the second security man. With Schelling in the middle, the trio ascended the steps to the front door.

There were eight steps as Mitchell counted them.

I'll let them take about three steps, he thought. Enough to be clear of the limousine, yet still short of the door.

The three entered the club and the doorman closed the door behind them. Mitchell let the branch fall back into place.

The security men would have to go too. . . . To leave them free to cut off his escape would be suicide. Mitchell didn't like it, but he knew he'd have to kill the three of them as they climbed the steps to the club entrance.

The Chancellor would be first, then the security man on the left . . . then on the right.

"Shit," Mitchell said softly to himself. He pushed the branch back one last time. The doorman was an old man . . . very old. Mitchell hoped the old man wouldn't accidently get in the way. If he didn't, nothing would happen to him.

Mitchell sat in the bushes until darkness had settled, then maneuvered his way back into the open. It was not something he was looking forward to. Still, it had to be done. The risks were there. He had a good plan, but he wasn't so naive as to be oblivious to the risks.

Two things bothered him specifically. What if another car pulled up at the club as the Chancellor and his party were getting out of the limo? The confusion in a situation like that might force him to postpone things for another week. The other possibility was that someone might be in the area of the bushes when he wanted to fire.

Whether he'd be able to fire three effective rounds didn't cross his mind. There was no question about that. And he determined he wouldn't worry about the other circumstances that he had no control over.

I'll be here next week, he thought, starting the cycle and driving northward out of the park. And I'll be ready.

Chapter 26.

Mitchell thought it wise to stay away from the Bundeskanzlerplatz. On thinking about it further, he decided he had a lot to risk by going outside at all. He could hardly believe that no one had picked up his trail by now. He had spent more time than was prudent in the Gouvernmental Quarter because it had been necessary. Now that he had the information he needed, he determined to leave his apartment on only the few occasions that were absolutely necessary.

Early Thursday morning, he walked to a shopping area near the apartment and picked up a week's supply of food, a dozen magazines, a light-weight pair of black leather gloves, a heavy duty needle and thread, scissors, a large thermos, and a duffel bag.

He watched TV until late that night. When the last local station signed off at three in the morning, Mitchell changed into a dark sweater and slacks, slipped the gloves in his hip pocket, and quietly left the apartment.

It was a still night, with a slight overcast that muffled the few sounds heard on the street. Mitchell drove unhurriedly into northwestern Bonn, where, during his first week in the city, he had spent several hours in carefully scrutinizing a variety of sporting goods shops.

The place he decided on was Albert's, an army surplus store of sorts with extensive but cluttered inventory and no apparent alarm system. The store was located in what was primarily a residential area, with a gas station and a small grocery store the only other businesses in the area. Mitchell parked a block and a half away and moved through the shadows of an alleyway to the back of the old frame structure that housed Albert's. Slipping on the gloves, Mitchell spent a moment to reassure himself that no alarm system was involved.

The lock on the back door was unsophisticated and it took less than a minute for him to maneuver the hook on the end of the tiny metal pick into the tumblers that snapped it open. Mitchell closed and locked the door behind him. There were two gun racks, as he remembered—one enclosed in glass on the wall, the other standing open in the center of the floor.

There were twenty-three guns in the floor rack, apparently placed there at random. Mitchell doubted that Albert himself, or whoever ran the place, had any idea of the actual number. The reflected light from a lamppost a half block away afforded him enough light to pick out a semi-automatic thirty caliber rifle from the end of the rack.

A car passed swiftly on the street outside and Mitchell froze momentarily in the shadows as it passed. He slid open a drawer behind the counter and fingered through the boxes of shells inside, holding them alternately up to the light until he came across the ones he needed. He took only one small box and closed the drawer.

Fifteen minutes after he had pulled up a block away from Albert's, Mitchell was starting his car and retracing his route to Bad Godesberg.

He slept late the next day. After he had wakened and

showered he took the rifle to the Drachenfels Sports Club, where he reluctantly met a half dozen well-meaning members who insisted he join them on the indoor rifle range.

After firing four rounds, Mitchell fabricated a reason to excuse himself. "I'm afraid the noise in here is a bit too much for me. I'm not used to these things."

The others assembled laughed good naturedly and slapped him on the back and said they understood. Of course they didn't.

Mitchell left them with an appropriately embarrassed look. Inside he felt quite smug. He had zeroed the weapon in two rounds. The other two, he fired at different points on the target so as to spread his pattern and not attract attention. Each of those rounds had ripped cleanly through its intended mark.

He spent part of the evening working on the easel case he had originally bought with his art supplies. Patiently ripping the stitches with a razor blade, Mitchell opened the seam, gaining two additional inches of width. He took great care in restitching it at its expanded size, overlapping the edges the smallest possible amount that would still insure the strength of the resewn fabric.

When he finished he looked approvingly at the case and then stood it on end with one hand, slipping the rifle inside with the other. It was snug, but the zipper worked freely. He closed it over the top and set the case with the rifle inside in his closet.

On Sunday afternoon he drove into the countryside west of Bonn. He left the car in a grove of trees a hundred yards off a rarely traveled country road and walked the several miles to the Belgian border. With the benefit of daylight, it was not a difficult route. Darkness he knew, would slow his rate somewhat. Still, it appeared there would be no major problems. He made mental notes as to guiding landmarks. He returned to Bonn in the late evening, satisfied he'd have no trouble making a quick, safe exit from Germany.

Frank Walker and Gustav Junger had been in Bonn for most of two weeks without a trace of Mitchell. Unknown to both them and Mitchell, they had passed within moments of one another on more than one occasion.

They sat in a hotel room late on Tuesday night after another frustrating day.

The pressure of time and their limitation in manpower had forced them to resort to the rather unsophisticated tactic of simply scouring the streets in the hopes of turning up Mitchell. They had nothing to go on but a computer printout and Walker's personal knowledge of Mitchell.

"Maybe he's gone," said Junger. "He may plan to be at a point where the Chancellor is visiting outside Bonn." Junger reached inside his jacket and removed a very sensitive document—a daily itinerary of the Chancellor's next two weeks. He studied it for a moment. "Next week the Chancellor will be in Amsterdam," he said.

Frank Walker didn't reply. He thought about Junger's point. He lit a cigarette and thought about it some more. The fact they hadn't found Mitchell weighed heavily on him. Walker believed Mitchell was in Bonn. But they had spent two weeks there with no sign of him. Walker tried once again to put himself inside Mitchell's mind.

"He could be anywhere by now," repeated Junger.

"Stop whining, dammit!" said Walker.

"I'm not," said Junger. "I'm simply saying he may be out of the country."

Walker shrugged. "You may be right. We've been pounding the streets and haven't turned up a thing. Maybe we've rushed on this a little too much. It might be a good idea to pull back and try another tact . . . dig into the I.D. thing." Walker thought on it a little longer. "His 'Werner' I.D.'s are too risky to use. There's no doubt he's replaced them." Walker sat up a little straighter in his chair. "We'd better run that down next."

"What do you think he might have used?"

"I don't know . . . a club card or two . . . a driver's license."

"We can check the new driver's license listings, see if any of them resemble him."

Walker perked up. "Go to Berchtesgaden tonight. He must have spent the night there the day before you found him. Try the out-of-the-way guest houses. See if we can get a name that matches his description. I'll check the records here on driver's license applications. If we come up with a name on both lists. . ."

Gustav Junger was walking out the door. "I'll call you as soon as I have something," he said.

Monday and Tuesday Mitchell waited. He read and re-read the magazines and newspapers. He watched TV and smoked.

The news of the assassination of Karl Stehlin had nearly run its course by now. An embarrassed government, still with no substantial leads, assured everyone that all possible angles were being investigated. The plain truth was they still hadn't turned up anything concrete to work on. The less the press had to say about it, the happier the government was.

They were a relatively long two days. Under the circumstances, Mitchell weathered them well.

Then, suddenly, it was Wednesday.

At the apartment, Mitchell packed scissors, mirror, hair coloring, shaving gear and two changes of clothing into the duffel bag. He filled the thermos with hot water and put both items in the trunk of the car.

At three in the afternoon, he left the apartment and drove the car to within eight blocks of the Schumann Club, parking in a small lot near another park along the east bank of the Rhine.

He walked easterly away from the lot for seven blocks, then caught a cab back to the apartment. As the cab crossed the Rhine and headed south, Mitchell once again reviewed his plan of escape.

He'd come to the park around five o'clock with his art equipment. The rules regarding the park apparently didn't prohibit small motorcycles, so he'd bring it into the park and set up in the proximity of the lilac bushes. The altered easel case would carry the rifle. When the opportunity presented itself, he'd slip the case into the bushes. Sometime between six and seven o'clock, he'd fold up his gear and move into the bushes himself.

And then, when the limousine pulled up, he'd do what he had to do.

After it was all over, he'd leave the rifle in the bushes and get out of the park on the motorcycle. Because of the distance and heavy foliage between his location and the club, and because of the vastness of the park and the relatively small number of people normally there, Mitchell hoped to be able to leave at a normal speed before anyone who might see him could realize what had happened.

He'd then drive the route he'd mapped earlier, approximately fifty kilometers from the Belgian border, where he'd ditch the car and set out on foot. When he got to within a few miles of the border, he'd shave, and cut and dye his hair. Then, after burying everything he'd

223

use to alter his appearance, he would cross the border into Belgium. The town of Eupen was another seven kilometers inside Belgium and there Mitchell would buy a train ticket to Brussels. How long he'd stay was something he'd decide later. From there, within a few hours time, he could move in any one of several directions into other countries.

Chapter 27.

At three o'clock on Wednesday afternoon, Frank Walker walked into the Bonn City Hall and identified himself as a research representative whose company was doing some work in the transportation area. He produced three supporting documents that he had had printed earlier in the day—a business card, a letter stating his purpose, and a brief questionnaire. "We're interested in how many people get new driver's licenses in a week's time . . . how old they are . . . whether they're men or women . . . the areas they live in . . . that sort of thing."

The clerk didn't think it was available.

"Would you mind if I look at some recent records? Say, those that have been issued in the past month or so?"

The clerk assured him it was impossible.

An appropriate amount of folded currency, slipped over the counter, carried far more influence than the official documents Walker had gone to the trouble of securing.

He left city hall an hour later with copies of a computer printout with over a thousand names, listed alphabetically, by the day of the month that the license had been issued.

Back in the hotel room, the phone rang at five o'clock.

"I have the names of eight people who stayed here that night that fit Werner's general description," said Junger. He began to read them off. Walker checked each name against each day on the computer printout.

"Franz Brandner," said Junger, halfway through his list.

Walker ran his finger down the page, flipping over the first few sheets.

Near the bottom of the next page, the name jumped out at him. "I think we've found our man," he said.

At five-thirty Mitchell put on the thin leather gloves and left the apartment for the last time. The easel case with the rifle inside, swung heavily at his side. He attached it, along with a few other art supplies to the motorcycle. Everything he had packed in the car, or carried with him on the motorcycle—from each single drawing pencil to the handlebars of the motorcycle, to the thermos, to the rifle—literally everything had been gone over painstakingly to assure that not a trace of a fingerprint would ever be found.

Frank Walker swore as the rush hour traffic of Bonn snarled the routes to Bad Godesburg. He inched along the traffic with what little patience he could muster.

At six o'clock, Frank Walker knocked on the door of Mitchell's apartment. His hand, slipped casually inside his pocket, was wrapped around a snub-nosed .38 caliber pistol.

Walker knocked a second and third time, then tried the door. To his surprise, it was unlocked.

Inside he found extra art supplies and a series of paintings and sketches of the Gouvernmental Quarter. So Mitchell *had* been in the Quarter. And apparently, quite often. From the perspective of the paintings, Walker could nearly pinpoint the spot from which Mitchell had worked.

The apartment had a look about it that indicated its occupant was not returning. The medicine cabinet was empty and drawers in the dresser were open and also empty.

Walker closed the apartment door and went to the office of the building.

"I'm an uncle of Franz Brandner," he said. "One of your tenants . . . Apartment 6. I'm in town on business and wanted to look Franz up. He seems to be out now. Would you have any idea where I might find him?"

The landlord was a friendly old man who was apologetic; he didn't know where Brandner was.

"I'll stop back a little later," Walker said. "Do you happen to know if he's still driving a black Volkswagen?"

"Yes, he is," said the landlord, happy to help. "That and his motorcycle."

"So he finally bought a motorcycle," Walker laughed. "He'd always threatened to do it."

"I think they're too dangerous myself. But young people today . . ." He threw up his hands. "What can you tell them?"

"What kind did he get?" asked Walker.

The old man shook his head. "I don't know much about them. It was a small one—red."

Walker laughed again. "Well at least he had enough sense not to buy a big one the first time around."

"Would you like me to tell him you called?" the old man asked.

"I'd like it to be a surprise," said Walker. "It's very

important that it be a surprise."

He left the apartment building. Neither the motorcycle nor the Volkswagen was in the parking lot. Walker headed for the Gouvernmental Quarter.

At nearly the same time, Mitchell parked the motorcycle near the clump of lilacs in the park. The traffic was heavier than it had been on the previous two occasions Mitchell had been there and he felt an irritation that things weren't exactly as he'd expected.

He took the sketch pad and sat cross-legged on the grass beside the lilac bushes. The "easel" lay beside him. He took one pencil from an inside pocket, opened the pad, removed his gloves and began to sketch the east side of the park.

He worked deliberately, slowly, and when he finished one sketch, he flipped the next page over with the tip of his pencil. The pencil would be the only thing with fingerprints on it, and Mitchell would wipe it clean before he left.

The restlessness in him settled as the clock moved past six-thirty. The number of people in the park had thinned considerably since his arrival. Many of them had probably been part of the normal after-work crowd that passed through the park on the way home or stopped there for a short relaxation after a long day. As on his previous visits, most of the activity in the park took place at the small pond in the northern end. Only one couple and a man walking his dog had passed nearby.

Mitchell checked his watch. Six-forty-five. He looked around the park in all directions. Slipping the gloves from his pocket, Mitchell put them on and with one quick movement slid the case into the opening in the bushes. He took the gloves off while rising from the ground to a standing position. He stretched his arms overhead and stood for a moment, then sat once again on the grass and began sketching absently. A slight breeze stirred through the bushes and Mitchell trembled and drew in a breath noisily. The traffic on the surrounding streets had quieted now from the rush hour. The park was nearly deserted.

Mitchell shuddered again and took a deep breath and exhaled loudly in an attempt to calm himself. He looked at his watch. Ten minutes after seven.

Walker searched the square and found no sign of either the car or the motorcycle. He was uneasy about the situation. The fact that Mitchell had apparently left the apartment for the last time indicated something significant was near at hand. Not seeing any sign of him in the quarter heightened Walker's apprehension.

Walker reached inside his jacket and pulled out the Chancellor's daily schedule. The next appointment was at the Schumann Club.

The name seemed familiar.

Walker looked back at the sheets from the previous two weeks. The same entry was on the schedule both weeks—seven-forty at the Schumann Club.

Walker ran to his car and headed north on Wilhelm-Spiritus-Ufer.

Mitchell stood and put the gloves on once again. He put the sketch pad in the carrying pouch on the motorcycle and fastened it. He took a final look around and seeing it was clear, scrambled into the bushes.

He took a few minutes to arrange himself on the inside and finally found a position with his back against several stout branches that provided the support he'd need. He drew his knees up with his feet flat on the ground and rested his arms across his knees as if they were the rifle. He'd fire from the sitting position.

He lifted his arm off his knee and pushed the branch back that opened the view to the Schumann Club. The doorman stood smoking, glancing down the Limpericher Strabe in both directions.

Mitchell released the branch and spent a moment wiping the prints from the pencil he'd been sketching with. Then he unzipped the case and worked the rifle out. The magazine was already locked and loaded to avoid the noise involved in that procedure. Mitchell had only to release the safety and fire. He raised the rifle to his shoulder, steadying his arms against his knees, and pushed the branch aside gently with the barrel.

The tip of the sight blotted out the head of the doorman at the Schumann Club.

Mitchell brought the rifle back down and cradled it across his lap. It was seven-twenty.

The blast of a ship's horn from the Rhine didn't penetrate Mitchell's consciousness at first.

It blew a second time, a harsh, hollow bellow that echoed along the river. It was the third blast before it occurred to Mitchell. The Kennedybrucke, his route out of Bonn, was a draw bridge! If a ship were passing and the goddamn bridge was up when he was trying to get away. . . He shrugged it off, but couldn't help feeling a little sick at the possibility.

No sooner had he dismissed thoughts of the draw bridge than Mitchell tensed at the sound of voices nearby. They came from behind him. Enclosed as he was, Mitchell couldn't risk the movement he would have to make to see what was going on. They were talking quietly, and Mitchell sensed they were very close. He strained to hear what they were saying.

"I don't see anybody around."

"You can't be too sure. There's a lot of trees around here."

They were the voices of two young men. Mitchell looked at his watch. Seven-thirty-five. What the hell were they doing!

"We won't be able to sell it for much," the first voice said. "Not in very good shape."

"We can always find somebody."

Mitchell's jaw set in anger. They were going to steal the motorcycle!

A million thoughts flooded his mind. What the hell do you do now?

"Wait a minute!" the first voice said. "Look!"

"Let's get out of here!"

Behind him Mitchell could hear the hurried steps of the two would-be thieves departing in the distance. He had no way of knowing what caused them to leave, and now, at seven-forty, he couldn't be concerned.

Mitchell raised the rifle to his shoulder and with the barrel pushed the branch aside. A car deposited a guest at the door of the Schumann Club and departed. Mitchell's breathing was steady and controlled now. The rifle at his shoulder seemed an extension of his body.

The blackness of the limousine was unmistakeable as it rolled up under the awning. Mitchell pushed his right thumb forward and the safety disengaged with a staccato "click."

Mitchell was totally immersed now as the door on the driver's side opened. The first security man stepped out and walked up the stairway to the club. So intent was Mitchell's concentration that the figure seemed close enough to touch. The image filled his mind as vividly as if it were being projected on a giant screen. He could fairly smell the odors and hear the final heart beats and last breaths from across the street as the first security guard came back down the steps and opened the rear door of the limousine.

The slightest pressure of his finger on the trigger was beginning to build.

He could nearly hear their footsteps on the carpeted stairway to the door.

"*Mitchell!*" the voice said.

It was a fierce whisper that resounded inside his head and nearly shattered his senses. He lowered the rifle in momentary confusion and it was then that he realized the sounds he'd heard in his intense concentration came from behind him. He began to whirl but the barrel of the rifle caught on the branches. The long arm from behind him shot out from the shoulder and caught him flush along the side of the jaw with the force of a mule's kick.

Mitchell felt the blow and heard the sickening crack of breaking bone. The force of it impelled him backward into the bushes. And in that split second before he lost consciousness, his eyes met the face behind the blow and his brain registered the familiarity of the voice.

Walker!

The few who saw them leave the park saw a tall man singing loudly and staggering along with a friend who'd obviously passed out draped around his shoulders. Everyone looked the other way and felt better when the tall man had finally dumped his friend in the back seat of his car and driven off.

Chapter 28.

Even before he opened his eyes, Mitchell knew he was in a hospital room. The antiseptic smell, while not unpleasant to him, was unmistakable. It penetrated his nostrils and began to reawaken his reluctant senses. After a few minutes, his eyes opened slowly to the white on white surroundings.

He lay there on his left side for several minutes staring at the blank wall and trying to get in touch with his faculties once again. His mind was clouded with a grogginess that was unfamiliar to him. He eventually realized he was unusually hungry. Other than that, he felt no discomfort. He finally moved an arm lethargically and flexed his fingers.

From across the room, the familiar voice boomed out. "I see you're finally awake."

Mitchell turned quickly in the bed and started to speak out when a stabbing pain and the wires that held his jaws firmly in place reminded him of the blow he'd taken.

"I hope you like milk shakes and soup," Walker said, getting off his chair and walking across the room. "I'm afraid that's all that will be on your menu for a while."

In a way, it was a relief to hear someone speaking in

English again. But considering the source, Mitchell hardly felt secure.

"Where the hell am I?" he demanded through clenched teeth. "And what the hell is going on?"

"It sounds like you're mad at me," said Walker, pulling up another chair near the bed.

Mitchell struggled to sit up in bed.

"Why don't you just take it easy and relax for a minute or two?" Walker asked. "The doctor says you'll be feeling fine in a few hours, but until then, there's no point in pushing yourself." Walker lit a cigarette and handed it to Mitchell. "I think I can understand your feelings. I'm sure you've got a lot of questions . . . I had a few myself . . . but I think you're going to feel a lot better after I set you straight on a few things."

Mitchell accepted the cigarette.

"First, I'm sorry about the jaw. I had no choice. But as you might have realized, it could have been worse— it could have been a lot worse." He paused for a moment and stared thoughtfully out the window. "The President thought we should kill you."

Mitchell's unaltered stare betrayed no emotion.

Walker stood and walked to the foot of the bed, continuing. "Only a handful of people knew anything about this operation. Only two people knew everything about it. I was one, the other was the President. After you bolted, we had a serious decision to make. Why had you taken off? Why not wait for instructions as you were told?"

Mitchell started to speak but Walker waved him off. "Two possibilities. Either you'd broken under the strain, or you felt you'd been set up to hit the wrong man. If you'd broken, we couldn't risk having you around to decide some day that you wanted to tell the world what happened." Walker looked Mitchell directly in the eyes. "The only reason you aren't dead now is because I believe you thought you were set up."

Mitchell finally spoke. "And if I believed you set me up then," Mitchell said, "how can I believe what you're saying now?"

Walker moved to a phone on a nearby table and dialed a number. "I have Mitchell here, sir," he said. Walker handed the phone to Mitchell.

"Hello."

There was no doubt of the identity of the voice on the other end of the line. "Hello, Mr. Mitchell. This is the President."

Mitchell sat dumbly as he continued.

"I understand your jaw isn't exactly fit for extended dialog but under the circumstances, this isn't a matter we want to discuss over the phone at length anyway. I'll get right to the point. Your mission was successful. We've accomplished what was necessary. Walker has convinced me of your dedication. We'll never be able to talk of this again; we owe you a dept we'll never be able to acknowledge. It must suffice to say that in behalf of the country, I am grateful."

"Thank you, sir," Mitchell managed to stammer.

The line clicked dead on the other end. Walker took the phone and replaced it on the table.

"That's one reason you can believe what I'm saying now," Walker said. "And after I explain the rest of the situation to you, I don't think you'll have a doubt left."

The relief Mitchell felt was so overwhelming he would have shouted if he could have opened his mouth.

"I hope the call helps to put you at ease," Walker said. "You probably feel a little rocky right now. We had to drug you to keep you under till we could get you out of the country and explain the whole situation to you."

"Where are we now?"

"Washington . . . Walter Reed."

"Walter Reed? My god, you really knocked me out!"

"I'm not surprised. It's been almost two days since we left Bonn."

"Two days!"

An Army nurse entered the room and motioned to Walker.

"I'm going to leave for a while now," he said. "They want you to eat and then nap for a few hours. They've given you a shot to counteract the drug we originally gave you. You'll get a couple of pills now and after an hour or two of sleep, you should be as good as new." Walker checked his watch. "It's nearly 1200 Hours now. I'll be back at 1900 and we'll go through this whole thing."

Mitchell didn't believe canned soup could taste so delicious. When the nurse left with the bowl he'd emptied for the third time, he lay there on the bed, relaxed for the first time in nearly three months.

At exactly seven o'clock, Walker tapped on the door of Mitchell's room and let himself in. Mitchell was sitting up in bed reading a magazine the nurse left with him.

"I must say you look a hell of a lot better," Walker said.

Mitchell laid the magazines aside. "I feel normal again—" he pointed to his jaw—"with this small exception."

"That shouldn't bother you too much longer. A couple of weeks, they tell me—maybe less—and you can take the wires off."

Walker slid one of the chairs near the bed and sat

down. "Well," he said, "I imagine you'd like to hear what happened."

"That's an understatement."

"I'll start it off by making one point. Then I'll try to answer all the questions you must have. The point I want to make is, Karl Stehlin *was* Big Red. You got the right man."

Mitchell gave a short ironical laugh. "If I had known that. . . ." His voice trailed off.

"Did you ever kill anyone you knew in the war?" Walker asked. He went on, answering the question himself. "Of course you didn't. The biggest single reason any soldier can kill an enemy in combat is because he's anonymous—he has no identity, no personality. If he knew who the other man was . . . if he knew about the other man's family and how he made his living and where he was from . . . it would be a hell of a lot harder. In this particular case, I felt it best that you didn't know. As far as I was concerned it would only complicate things for you, make it harder for you to function. The anonymity kept you from worrying about all the things you eventually had to worry about when you found out who he was. You had enough on your mind without that."

"I suppose you're right."

"So after it happened and you turned up missing, I had to make a quick decision on what to do about you." Walker clasped his hands behind his head and leaned back in the chair. "As I said earlier, I figured either you'd cracked under the strain or you thought you'd been set up. Finally, I settled on the last idea. And judging from what we stopped you from doing in Bonn, I apparently was right."

"You were right," Mitchell affirmed. "There were just too many little pieces that didn't fall into place.

237

I believed I'd been used."

"What were the things that bothered you?"

"By themselves, most of them didn't seem too important. In fact they were little things I really hadn't noticed. I guess it was only when I couldn't believe Karl Stehlin was the real target that they seemed to fit together to raise more questions." Mitchell turned and fluffed his pillow and sat up straighter in bed. "I guess the first thing was the fact the original letter came from OPAIS. It seemed to me later, considering the sensitivity of the thing, that no chance would be taken that anyone would remember a communication like that."

Walker started to answer, but Mitchell went on.

"And when I thought back on our meeting at the Federal Building in Chicago, it was as if you really didn't belong in there, almost like you'd broken in and used the place just for my benefit to convince me you were really connected with the government. And the security guard—he was too sharp when I thought back on it." Mitchell pictured the man again in his mind. "No," he said, "he was no security guard; he was a soldier."

"You're partly right," Walker said. "We borrowed an office from one of our good friends—he didn't know why and of course we wouldn't tell him. We exercised quite a bit of care to see that you got in and out as inconspicuously as possible. That's why we picked a time when we knew the Loop would be as close to deserted as it ever gets." Walker smiled. "And yes, we had one of our men acting as security guard to help in that respect."

Mitchell went on to the next point.

"The classification marking that I saw later on the orders—when we were in Colorado—that bothered me too," Mitchell said. "I'd never seen one like it before."

"All orders for our department are classified by me. I can put on any restriction that's needed to qualify it. In this specific case, I even typed the whole thing myself. No one else ever saw it." He rested his legs on the lower railing of the bed and waited for the next question.

"The M-16," Mitchell said. "Why use an American weapon—why leave it behind?"

"If you were one of the world's greatest shots with a German Mauser or a Soviet AK-47, we'd have used one of those," said Walker. "We used the M-16 because that was the weapon you were totally familiar and accurate with. We left it behind because it would have slowed your getaway or someone might have seen you leaving Peterskirche with a weapon—which would surely have attracted more attention than if you were unarmed—and finally, to leave the M-16 made it appear that the act probably wasn't commited by an American. It doesn't seem likely that an American would use an American weapon and then make no effort to conceal or destroy it. So, leaving the weapon actually added to the little confusion."

The next question caught Walker off guard.

"What about Gustav Junger?"

"How do you know his name?"

Mitchell felt a satisfaction at having picked up something Walker hadn't known he was aware of. "I pieced it together from something you told me and something I overheard." He took a cigarette pack off the table, offered one to Walker and took one himself. "He was my contact, wasn't he?"

"Yes," said Walker, lighting both cigarettes, "he was."

"When I read that he'd died, it shook me up. I thought I was next." Mitchell looked directly at Walker. "What happened?"

"Nothing."

"Nothing? Can you elaborate on that a little?"

"Gustav Junger was a name someone was using just as you were using Eric Werner. After Junger had completed his main task—setting everything up—we arranged for a fire to wipe out all traces of him. He helped me look for you. He's the man you lost at the airport in Munich, and later in the mountains outside Berchtesgaden."

"That was Junger! My God!" said Mitchell. "He told me that. When he was chasing me, he yelled it out." Mitchell shook his head. "I couldn't believe him. Where is he now?"

"He left the country under new identification." Walker pulled a wallet from an inside pocket and opened it to a passport with Mitchell's photo on it. "We had the same kind of cover for you. We'd planned to get you out, then arrange the accident for Eric Werner that you may have read about later." He inhaled deeply and the smoke escaped from his lungs as he talked. "When you disappeared, we waited a couple of days and then staged the Werner accident anyhow. The object of both 'deaths' was to forever remove those two from any scrutiny that might later tie them to the assassination. Also, we were looking like hell for you and by making you officially dead, we were pretty well assured that no one else would be trying to beat us to you."

"When I heard that report on TV," Mitchell said, "I thought it was the clincher—I was expendable."

"I guess you would have been expendable if that's what we'd wanted . . . but as you know now, we just wanted to get you back."

Mitchell thought a moment before he spoke. "Walker?"

Walker anticipated the question. "Whose bodies turned up in the accidents?"

Mitchell nodded.

Walker shrugged. "We'll slip one out of a morgue or off a floor in some skid row flop house."

"That easy, huh?"

"No!" Walker snapped. "It isn't easy! Nothing in this business is." Walker got to his feet and strode across the room to a window that faced a passing side street. "It's necessary." He shrugged again, looking out the window. "You do whatever is necessary for the success of the mission, whether it's personally distasteful to you makes no difference. You do whatever is necessary."

It was as close to losing his composure as Walker would ever come. They didn't speak for a moment. Mitchell smoked his cigarette and Walker stared fixedly out the window.

"Well," he said finally, "what else is on your mind?"

"The phone number."

"Oh, yes—the phone number. After the mission was accomplished we had it disconnected. It was set up in case an emergency arose before the project could be carried out. We didn't want any calls on the line afterward. It was a private number and anyone who called it would be told it never existed." Walker turned away from the window and looked back at Mitchell. "Nothing traceable—that's the goal. I'm sure you thought about that when you had your doubts too. Not one single thing to trace you to us, including the phone number. You see," said Walker, "we had to be prepared for any eventuality. If you were caught or killed—" He held up his hands in a gesture of helplessness—"there's no way we could be tied to you."

The answers to what Mitchell thought had been perplexing questions seemed embarassingly logical now. He felt a little uncomfortable for having assessed things so incorrectly. Still, a few more points had to be cleared up.

"What about Schelling?"

"What about him?"

"You know what I mean. He was there that night. You couldn't take the chance that Stehlin wouldn't sit in the chair on the left. Someone had to guarantee it. Schelling had to be in on it."

"Oh, come on, Mitchell," Walker scoffed. "No one tells the Chancellor of West Germany where he sits to eat dinner. He sits where he damn well pleases." Walker moved back across the room and sat down once again in the chair. He held up the fingers of his left hand and tapped them with his right index finger as he made his points. "Karl Stehlin had been in Irmgard's fifteen times during the last year. Fifteen times he sat at the same table. Fifteen times he sat in the same chair. We took the odds. If someone else had sat in the chair on the left that night they'd be dead now and Karl Stehlin would be spending a lot of time looking over his shoulder." Walker butted his cigarette out. "Next question."

"I saw an article in the paper—a small one—regarding a conspiracy. . . ."

"Right," said Walker. "Frau Reichert." He shook his head. "Whoever it was that talked to her husband had apparently found out the same thing we did."

"Won't that publicity provoke some thought?"

"We've kept a finger on it. No one takes it very seriously. The best thing about her report was the fact there was no mention of the group being composed of independently operating cells. Whether their source or Herr Reichert knew about it is anyone's guess, but apparently Frau Reichert didn't. Any member of any cell that read the report would have no way to relate it to his own group. And the only people in each cell who knew Stehlin's real purposes knew that their cell had nothing to do with his death. I don't think we have anything to worry about from them," Walker said. "All the activity within those cells was set up and strictly regulated by Stehlin. *Nothing* was undertaken without his guidance. With him gone, the cells are unorganized and without direction. I'm confident in a matter of time a lot of them will disband. And if they do continue to exist, it will be as an individual local unit that won't pose any threat to the government."

"I guess it falls into place now." Mitchell wanted to defend himself. "You can see how I might have jumped to the wrong conclusion though, can't you, Walker?"

"Mistakes like you made can be fatal in this business, Dave. But I think you've learned something." Walker smiled. "If you would have trusted me, if you would have waited till we contacted you, you'd have been lying in the sun somewhere four weeks ago—without a broken jaw."

"O.K.," Mitchell said resignedly. "I made a mistake."

"The point is, are you straight now?"

Mitchell thought. Somewhere in the back of his mind lingered another obscure question. He couldn't put his finger on it at the moment. It must not be very important, he thought. Everything he'd heard made sense. "I'm straight," he said.

Walker pressed the button beside the bed and almost instantly a nurse in a crisply starched uniform came into the room carrying a small suitcase. Walker thanked her and snapped the case open. Inside was a small assortment of men's clothing.

"For you," Walker said. "No sense staying in here if you don't have to."

"You mean they'll release me already?"

"Doctor says for you to watch the jaw. In three weeks, wherever you're at, go to a hospital and get the wires taken out. He said you shouldn't have any problems."

Mitchell was already out of bed and ruffling through the suitcase. "What now?" he asked as he pulled on a pair of slacks.

Walker reached inside his jacket pocket and took out an envelope. "I've got a couple of things here for you." He handed the contents to Mitchell. The first thing Mitchell noticed was the cash.

"A thousand dollars," Walker said.

The other item was an airline ticket.

"Rio de Janiero," said Walker. "It's a nice place for a vacation. People tend to mind their own business there, including the police. You'll be able to unwind there without worrying about anything."

"How long do I stay in Brazil?"

"Until you get tired of it." Walker took a pen from his jacket and wrote something across a scrap he tore from a newspaper on the table. "This is a bona fide working phone number. All I ask is that when you move, let me know where you'll be."

"When will you want me again?"

"It's hard to say . . . could be a few weeks . . . could be a few years. Just relax and enjoy life. We'll let you know when we need you. We'll make two fifty-thousand-dollar deposits to your Swiss account every year whether we get together or not. It's automatic."

Mitchell had finished dressing. Walker pulled yet another group of items from an outside coat pocket. "Here's a new identity for you . . . passport . . . driver's license . . . the works."

Mitchell looked at it carefully. "John Randall, huh?"

"Ready to leave this place, Jack?"

They walked out of the room and down the corridor and out the door into the gathering dusk.

"How did you find me?" Mitchell asked. "How did you know what I was up to?"

"Hard work," said Walker, "together with what I knew about you. And a little help from a computer that figured some odds for us. We got our first trace on you when you made that call from outside Berchtesgaden to the disconnected phone number. When you called that night, we were able to pinpoint your location. Junger was down there the next morning, as you found out."

Walker told Mitchell the rest of the story while they walked to the parking lot. When they got to Walker's car, he was finishing up.

"And when I saw the park, I figured that's where you must be. I saw the motorcycle there and took off running toward it. All of a sudden, I saw two boys running away from the area. I almost started to follow them. But as I got to the bush, I heard a click that was probably your safety being released."

"The boys you saw were going to steal my bike," said Mitchell. "I wondered at the time what had frightened them away."

Walker had finished. "And you know the rest."

Mitchell shook his head in wonder. "I don't know why I should be surprised," he said. "The whole operation was incredible from the very beginning. I guess there's no reason why it shouldn't have ended the same way."

Walker thrust his hand out. "I probably won't see you for awhile, Dave. Take care of yourself. You did a good job. Now that you know a little more about how we operate, it should be easier next time."

They shook hands and Mitchell doubted if that kind of work could ever be easy. Walker got inside the car and closed the door.

"Have a good time in Rio," he said, starting the car.

The question Mitchell had searched his mind for earlier in the hospital room had surfaced as they stood talking in the parking lot and he wondered why he hadn't asked it before now. Walker had put the car in gear and was ready to pull out of the lot.

"Walker," Mitchell said, "going back to that night at Irmgard's. Granted that Stehlin always sat at the same chair at the same table, how could we know he'd be there at that time on that night?"

Walker studied the instrument panel on the car as Mitchell spoke. After a moment's hesitation he looked up.

"The answer to that one, Dave—and I guess you might as well know—the answer is. . . ." He hesitated again for a moment and then went ahead as if he had resigned himself to saying it. "You were right about that part—Frederich Schelling set it up."

Mitchell stood dumbly as the white Dodge rolled out of the lot and onto the street. In a moment it was gone.

Mitchell walked aimlessly for a half hour and finally hailed a cab. "Dulles Airport, please."

He settled back in the cab. So the new Chancellor of West Germany wasn't guilty of being a Communist or a Nazi or a Fascist. All he'd done was to arrange the assassination of the former Chancellor. Mitchell wondered what kind of deals had been made. Perhaps the man truly acted in the best interest of his country; perhaps he'd acted in his own self-interest.

And what about the United States government stake in the situation? Perhaps it had acted strictly in the best interests of the free world; perhaps it had acted in its own self-interest.

Mitchell was certain he'd never know the answers to those questions and he wasn't entirely certain that he cared to. The implications, as they say, could be staggering.

He thought about it for a minute and dismissed it

from his mind. Worrying about it would make absolutely no difference in what would eventually transpire. He'd accept what he'd been told and considered that all involved parties had acted to resolve the situation in the best interests of the free world.

Forget it, he thought.

He wondered if his broken jaw would keep him from scoring in Rio.

Darkness had settled firmly now and as the cab penetrated the night toward Dulles International, Mitchell became aware that his hands were cold and he shivered at the chill that seemed to fill the cab. The temperature outside, he thought, which had been quite comfortable when he stood talking with Walker, must have cooled very suddenly.

He pulled his jacket closer about him and reached over to roll the window up.

It was already closed.

CHARTER BOOKS
Suspense to Keep You
On the Edge of Your Seat